Ten Years to Bangkok

A True International Love Story

Edwin Kime

Ten Years to Bangkok ~ A True International Love Story

Copyright © 2004 Edwin Kime All Rights Reserved

Cover design by Rebecca Hayes

Editing by Amanda Hafner

Layout by Rebecca Hayes

Published in the United States by
Cedar Hill Publishing
P.O. Box 905
Snowflake, Arizona 85937
http://www.cedarhillpublishing.com

Library of Congress Control Number 2004109935

ISBN 1-932373-81-0

DEDICATION

I wish to dedicate this book to all the people who have helped me with its writing. The book was actually started in 1990, and was originally done in long-hand. During my many moves and the 1991 Gulf war some of the pages were lost. It was finally completed, and the lost pages rewritten, when we traveled to Thailand, in 2003, to help care for my wife's sick mother.

The winter of 2003 and spring of 2004 were used to move the book from handwritten pages to the computer. I want to express special thanks to my wife and my sister who spent many hours reviewing and editing the book for me. Special thanks to all the people who put up with me during the writing process. Also to our children who helped us and most of all to my parents who made it all possible.

Table of Contents

Chapter 1: On the Way 1
Chapter 2: Bangkok Arrival 7
Chapter 3: The Start of the Trip 11
Chapter 4: The Search for Emma 16
Chapter 5: Bangkok Sights 26
Chapter 6: A Night Out 31
Chapter 7: Pattaya 50
Chapter 8: Back to Bangkok 70
Chapter 9: Another Beginning 84
Chapter 10: Back to Work 99
Chapter 11: Return to Bangkok 117
Chapter 12: Singapore, Here We Come 129
Chapter 13: Bangkok, We Are Back 140
Chapter 14: A Trip to Phuket 144
Chapter 15: Bangkok, Again 156
Chapter 16: The Trip to the Village 161
Chapter 17: Back at Bangkok 169
Chapter 18: The Start of Dow's U.S. Visa 174
Chapter 19: USA, Here We Come 181
Chapter 20: Travel in the USA 185
Chapter 21: Our Separate Ways 198
Chapter 22: Dow's Panama Flight 204
Chapter 23: The Search 206
Chapter 24: The Marriage 218

Chapter 1: On the Way

It was May 1978 at the Dhahran International Airport in Saudi Arabia; I was trying to make my flight for my R&R to Thailand. It was the normal hot dry desert air, and everybody was sweating and pressing to enter into the terminal. After getting inside the Airport terminal, I rushed toward the Gulf Air terminal check-in counter. The smell of the sweat attempted to be masked by perfume on the Arabs; however, the body odor came through and made for an even more unpleasant odor as I tried to make my way to the check-in counter. The traditionally clad Arabs and the Asians all waiting and wishing to get a flight out of Saudi Arabia held up the people who had scheduled tickets.

I had come early to get an 8:00PM flight to Bahrain, so that if I missed or was bumped on that flight, I still had a chance to get the 10:00PM flight, which was always overbooked. I waited in line as the Arabs tried to reach over my shoulder with their tickets with an extra 100 Saudi riyals or even 400 Saudi riyals in between the pages of the plane tickets to get on the flight. I was pushing and shoving to hold my place in the line that seemed to change with whoever was at the check-in counter taking the tickets. The line slowly inched forward to the ticket counter. Finally, after what seemed like hours, I reached the ticket counter and gave the Gulf Air clerk my tickets to get my boarding pass.

He eyed me carefully and said, "How many bags will you be checking?"

"Only one bag," I answered him, handing him my black bag to be checked in. He went through the same ritual, stamping and stapling the tickets and the boarding pass and putting the tag on the checked baggage along with the ID number, as well as inside the ticket folder. "Please check the bag all the way to Bangkok," I asked the clerk. With a grunt, he answered me with "Yes, I will do that". After all the papers were in place, he handed me back my tickets, boarding pass, and baggage slip.

"Be at the gate early," he added, as he took back the packet for one last look to ensure that all items were there.

I turned to thank Tony and Bill, who had brought me to the airport to catch my flight. I was thinking how nice it is to have my good friends help. I met Tony while I was working in Khamis, and when that project finished, I was able to get him and J. C. Moore reassigned to the project I was on at Ras Tanura. Being good workers, I knew they would be a help to the project since there were so many inexperienced people on the project already.

Tony said, "Well, you have fun in Thailand."

Then Bill added, "Don't do anything that I wouldn't do."

"Gee! That really left the gate open," I replied. At that time, the ticket clerk walked toward the departure gate. Then there was a stampede of people after him. I quickly moved with the stampeding people, waving goodbye to Tony and to Bill as I moved toward the immigration counter.

Then I arrived at the immigration check out counter, where I waited in line with the other people. However, some Saudis cut the line and pushed to the front and were not sent back by the immigration officers. Finally, I made it to the counter and gave my passport to the immigration officer. He flipped through the pages of my passport, although the exit reentry visa was marked by a paperclip. Finally, he returned to the paper-clipped page and started stamping the passport and the exit card. Then he handed it back to me as I hurried away to the boarding gate for the Gulf Air flight.

I have always had an empty feeling as I have headed out toward something new and unknown. Going to a place I have never been, I experienced a thrill, yet an uncertain feeling gripped me as I moved toward the unknown.

Finally, the departure gate opened and the pushing and shoving started again as the line moved through the departure gate. The air was hot as we left the terminal and walked toward the waiting plane. The plane ride from Dhahran to Bahrain is only five minutes on the prop plane. The prop on opposite the side we were boarding was already running. The noise of the running engine and the air hurt my ears as I started up stairs to board the plane. I quickly found my assigned seat, however most sat were they pleased, then sat down, and fastened my seat belt as I glanced out the plane window. All the lights that were on at the airport cast a tan colored light through a cloud because of all the sand in the air. However, the sky was almost cloudless above.

The stewardess passed quickly among the passengers handing out candy as the last passengers entered the plane, and the door was closed for the flight. The other plane engine was started as the stewardess informed the passengers of the safety procedures. The second engine was getting up to the proper RPMs as the plane started taxiing toward the runway. Finally, we were at the runway and an announcement came to the stewardess to be seated, as we were ready for take off. The lights were dimmed and the plane raced down the runway to get the proper speed for lift off. As the plane lifted off from the runway and gained altitude, the lights from Bahrain were visible. (The flight from Saudi Arabia to Bahrain is only 5 to 7 minutes depending on if the plane is a prop or a jet the jet taking longer on the short flight.)

It seemed like seconds as the plane reached altitude and then had to start its descent to the airport in Bahrain. The lights became brighter as we started our approach to the airport in Bahrain. The touchdown was smooth and we quickly started our approach to Bahrain airport. The plane slowed then taxied up to the terminal and came to the usual bumpy stop at the gate. Finally, the plane door was opened and the people exited the plane to the terminal.

I joined the stream of people that was headed for the transit lounge and the check-in counter for transit passengers. I waited in the line to confirm my flight out to Bangkok on Singapore Airlines. Finally, it was my turn to pass the clerk my tickets to get my boarding pass. I handed the agent my tickets and he slowly checked the list to confirm my ticket. Then he printed out my boarding pass and gave me the gate to catch my flight. With the usual "be at the gate early", he returned my ticket and my new boarding pass. I was ready for the flight.

I went to the airport lounge and ordered two beers. I found a seat by the window looking over the incoming planes and sat down. I opened one beer and it tasted really good. I had not had one for five months while I was working in Saudi Arabia. Many of the people were headed to the duty free shop after getting their boarding passes. This group was now arriving at the lounge with their bottles. They bought mixers in the lounge and the seats were filling up so they could mix and enjoy their drinks. The only empty seat left was at the table where I sat.

"Mind if I join you?" ask one of the latecomers.

"No," I answered. "I have to catch the 2:00AM flight to Bangkok so will be leaving shortly."

"You flying to Bangkok, too?" came his rely as he poured himself a drink containing two-thirds Jim Beam and one-third Pepsi mixer.

"Yes," I answered, as I was finishing my first beer. "Were you working?" I asked as I started on my second beer.

"Oh, I work in Ras Tanura," he responded to my question. He finished the first glass and mixed himself another drink that almost emptied the Jim Beam bottle.

"I work in Ras Tanura also," I answered him. As I was well into my second beer, I added, "It is too bad they don't allow this in Saudi Arabia." After a short pause of silence, we talked about work and enjoyed the drinks. I asked him what project he worked on; but, getting no response, I dropped the subject.

The Arab group that had come on the earlier Gulf Air flights spent their time drinking in the lounge and hurried to catch the last flight to Dhahran as it was announced. It was quite a shaky crew wandering down the hall with their drinks to the departure gate.

Then the announcement came about boarding my flight and I left for the boarding gate. My tablemate was emptying the Jim Beam bottle as I left for the gate.

I reached the boarding gate and waited in the line. Finally, when it was my turn, I gave my boarding pass to the agent and boarded the plane. I found my seat and got ready for the flight and to get some sleep. As the other passengers found their seats, the flight was almost ready to leave. Then came the Jim Beam man, who could hardly stand up. When he passed me, I got up and helped him; I found his boarding pass and his assigned seat number and helped him to his seat, as I was afraid the stewardess would kick him off the plane. I struggled with him to get him into his assigned seat, fastening his seat belt as he fell asleep, just as a stewardess walked by to check on him. I got back to my seat and settled in as they were doing the last minute checks before the 747 backed out from the gate. Last minute checks completed, they closed the doors and backed out away from the boarding gate. Finally, we were taxiing to the runway for takeoff.

Slowly the huge 747 turned onto the runway. After a moment's pause on the runway, the plane crept slowly forward at first, then gained speed quickly and finally lifted off as the lights of Bahrain passed under us and out of sight.

The plane leveled out as the seatbelt sign was turned off. The stewardess started moving around the plane. Suddenly, the Jim Beam man pushed a $20 bill into the hand of the stewardess saying, "Bring me two more Jim Beams and a Coke." After a short time, the stewardess returned with the two Jim Beams and the Coke. He hurriedly finished the first drink, then quickly poured himself the second bottle. He swiftly finished it and fell instantly into a deep sleep as the 747 turned and corrected its flight path toward Bangkok. Most passengers started to fall asleep in the early morning hour as the 747 sped on its way to Bangkok.

Chapter 2: Bangkok Arrival

The Singapore Airlines Boeing 747 from Bahrain dipped its right wing as it corrected its flight path to land at Bangkok International Airport. From out the window, I could see the country freshly washed from the morning rain and sparkling like diamonds where the leaves and other places held the raindrops. The gold and colored roofing tile atop the Buddhist temple shone in the morning sunshine like a strange kingdom, very different from the just departed desert kingdom. The temple looked more like a fairy tale place than a real place. With its white walls and red roof tile and the high gold gables on the roof, it looked like a building fit to house Gods.

The plane leveled, hiding the temple from view, with its surrounding banana and coconut trees and flooded rice fields with the green shoots coming up.

Then came the usual sound of the stewardess saying, "We are approaching Don Muang International Airport; please bring your seats to the upright position, buckle your seat belts and put your tables and trays away for landing." The plane powered down like a silver swan to a wet runway, splashing water as the tires hit the puddles. The tires made a mist as they hit the water on the runway, and the sun shone through the mist causing rainbows to form as we taxied down the runway to the airport. The braking engines slowed the big silver bird to a slow, controllable speed as we moved along the runway. We made the turn from the runway to the taxiway and the approach to the terminal. We finally taxied up to the gate and the final locking of the brakes stopped the plane at the gate.

The usual rush to get through immigration is always a hassle, I thought to myself as I made my way through the long corridors and finally came out to the immigration section to get into a line with five people in front of me. After the people in front of me had their passports checked and it was finally my turn, I passed my passport through the slotted area at the booth to the immigration officer. I said "Sawaddi" to the officer handing him my passport, and very politely, he returned my greeting with a bowed head, saying "Sawaddi" with a wai—the clapping of the hands, which can be from the chest to the head depending on the person being greeted.

The strange writing on the window was very different to me. How strange it seemed to me, being nothing like English, Japanese, or Chinese, or the writing in Europe that I have seen. The immigration officer was very pleasant and I was thinking how the American immigration officers could learn from these people. The officer stamped the cards and the passport as he looked at me to confirm the picture on the passport. Then, with a smile, he handed back to me the stamped passport and said, "Have a pleasant stay in Thailand." I picked up the passport and moved quickly to the baggage claim area.

I found the correct baggage claim area, then started looking for my luggage. The circular conveyor seemed to be slow in passing out the mix of all different shapes and colors of baggage. I waited and waited for my suitcase but it did not come. Shortly, all the suitcases had been unloaded from the plane and I still did not have my suitcase. I finally found a representative from Singapore Airlines and filed the necessary lost luggage claim. I selected the kind of luggage lost and provided them my baggage claim ticket. They told me they would bring my luggage to my hotel tomorrow. The tour I had scheduled included the airline, the New Amarin Hotel, and some in-country tours. Singapore Airlines provided me some Thai money to buy shaving gear, toothbrush, and toothpaste until my luggage arrived the next day. I realized why it is so important to always carry on luggage with the necessary articles in it.

I proceeded to the customs checkpoint without any baggage. I was closely watched since I did not have any baggage. I provided the customs officers with the lost luggage slip and they asked, "Did you only have one suitcase?"

I answered, "Yes, I only had one suitcase." Then they motioned over the Singapore Airlines representative. They talked to him in Thai. Then the representative rushed off and came back with a courtesy kit for me. Then the customs officers smiled and let me move through customs.

I stopped at the exchange bank at the airport and exchanged $100 into Thai money, called baht. I got 20 baht for one US dollar, making me feel rich giving the banker $100 and getting back 2000 baht. I wanted to have some money for tips and all and would exchange more at the banks in town, where I believed the rates would be better.

When I got through customs, I looked carefully for the tour agent, but I was unable to find the tour after waiting so long for the luggage. I walked back and got a Thai Airlines taxi to go to the hotel. I found my taxi, got into the back seat, and told the driver what hotel to head for. Then we started for the hotel. The driver asked the usual questions, such as where was I from, and I answered the United States.

"Is this your first visit to Thailand?"

"Yes," was my answer. I looked through my passport holder for the piece of paper with directions on it. I found it written out in English.

Emma Bhamorabutr
From Victory monument take
Raichawithi road, take the first
road left. I live in the seventh
house on the second floor.
The landlord lives on the ground floor.

I carefully read the paper again. An airman from the Thai Royal air Force gave these directions to me ten years ago in Saigon. I got these directions from the airman, whose name was Emma, at Saigon's Tan Son Nhut Airport. We had met in Saigon and we talked and drank beer. I had helped him get some toys for his kids and some Jack Daniels and Salem cigarettes to take back to Thailand with him. While I was waiting to be sent back north to Da Nang and he was headed back to Thailand, I gave him my address and he gave me directions to his house. I figured neither of us expected that we would ever meet again. Each of us wanted to visit the other's country as we talked about it, and about Viet Nam and the heat, and about Thailand.

He was married and had two sons and a daughter, and they were eager for him to return. Finally, it was time for me to leave, and we shook each other's hands and wished each other good luck, and traded the addresses before leaving. We promised to find the other if we ever came to the other's country.

I was thinking of asking the taxi driver if he knew of this location when we pulled in front of the hotel. *I've got two weeks to find him,* I thought to myself. I slowly slid out of the taxi and was thinking all the time how this trip came about so far away from here and so long ago; this trip to Bangkok actually started over ten years ago in Viet Nam.

Chapter 3:
The Start of the Trip

My 1955 yellow Chevrolet pickup with the homemade camper had pulled to a stop at the tile warehouse. I got out and started up to the coffee area at the warehouse when two strange men in suits approached me outside of the warehouse and called my name. Thinking they were from the court, I tried to avoid them. The suits made them look like Wall Street executives at a McDonalds; at the ceramic tile warehouse, they were really out of place. Seeing no way to get away from them, I turned toward them. In very stern voices, they tried their best to scare me. They flashed some sort of IDs at me and then started in to explain to me that they were here because I had failed to reregister for the draft after my divorce. They looked like salesmen from some kind of horror show that nobody would watch.

Then they threw their best sales pitch. "We can bring you in now and have you sent to Viet Nam for breaking the law—did you know that?" That was the first threat they let fly to scare me. Time stood still for a split second. Then they passed out a couple more threats.

Satisfied that their job was done, they walked away leaving their ugly scars and hatred behind.

Being early is not a blessing to a draft physical. The people came in all shapes and sizes. The room was really overcrowded. Finally, everybody was seated and ready to start the testing and a quiet fell over the room like the silence at a funeral. Suddenly, the testing silence was broken by the entrance of three army-uniformed people into the room. A very quick explanation, the required programmed speech, was given by one of the Army soldiers of the test we were to take, and then they passed out the test and the pencils. One of the soldiers said, "Start." Most of the people started filling out the test the best that they could. I had opened my test and was working very hard to do the very best I could on the test.

Then a strange sound came from the corner of the room and everybody turned around to look. There sat an overweight man tearing apart the test into long narrow strips. As he finished tearing the strips, he put the strips into his mouth and ate them. Quickly, two uniformed men came into the room and escorted the man out of the room.

Badly shaken, I returned to the test. The room had almost quieted down again when another person in the room fell onto the floor and was rolling around on the floor, yelling, kicking, and screaming as loud as he could. Again, the uniformed people came into the room and dragged the man out while he was kicking and screaming.

The room was returning to silence when a loud laugh broke out. This time a man was making paper airplanes from the examination papers and sailing them toward the front of the room, and everybody started laughing about that. Then the usual routine of the two uniformed people coming in to escort out the offender commenced.

The time was finally up on the timed examination. The people came in to collect the tests we had finished. It was time to move to the next part of the examination.

Like lambs to slaughter, we were herded into another room. We were given the usual speech before we started the physical: how everybody needed to do the best they could to get the best position when they were drafted. The man in front of me turned to me and asked if I wanted to urinate in his cup. I politely refused, and when I did, he quickly produced a small bottle of Johnny Walker and poured some of it into his cup. Then he urinated into the cup and finished off the bottle of Johnny Walker "to help me with my physical," he said. As the line moved on, clothes were taken off. Finally down to just jockey shorts, the physical continued. The medics checked for all sorts of things: hemorrhoids, hernias and—it seemed like—everything else in the book. After all the checks came the final line up to talk to the doctor, with everyone in their shorts.

The line up was long; I waited behind the line on the floor to be called by the doctor for my talk. The man in front of me was called by the doctor. Then I stepped up to the line so I could be next. I could hear the doctor talking to the man who was in front of me. The man was telling the doctor "I just had an appendix operation so I will not be able to go into the service till it is fully healed." He explained his condition to the doctor. The doctor finished looking at him and asked him, "When did you have the appendix operation?" Before the man could answer, the doctor explained, "Because you do not have any scar from the operation." Before the man could speak again, the doctor yelled out "Next!" and the man walked away, shaking his head.

Since it was my turn, I stepped up to the doctor, who had very dirty glasses. In a very bitter tone the doctor asked, "Well, what is wrong with you?"

I looked back and answered him by saying, "Nothing that I know of."

"What?" came his surprised reply. Then before anything else was said, he yelled, "Next!" And I walked away.

Glad that the testing and physical were all over, I quickly got dressed and finally got out of that mad house.

Then one of the interns came to me and said I had high blood pressure. He informed me, "You will have to come back twice a week for three weeks to have your blood pressure checked by us."

"NO!" came my reply. I said I would not do that.

A surprised look came over his face. "Well, I can have you shipped out right now to Viet Nam!" he screamed at me.

"Well, do it," I answered back to him. I was tired of being threatened with being sent to Viet Nam all the time.

The intern backed away from his threat and said, "How about laying down on the cot in the other room for 15 minutes and I will recheck your blood pressure, and if it is alright, we can end this."

I lay down on the cot, resting and staring at the dirty ceiling. I could hear the interns playing poker in the other room. I heard the rustle the man made as he returned to recheck my blood pressure. "Ready to try again," he said as he entered the room with the meter to check my blood pressure. Quickly, he placed the band around my arm to recheck the blood pressure. I could feel the band tighten as he pumped the bulb on the meter. He wanted to get back to his poker game as quickly as possible. "It's okay," he said. "You're on your way to Viet Nam," he said jokingly. "Go on, get out of here" There could not have been better words for me to hear. I was glad it was over and I would not have to go through that again.

I joined the Seabee's to keep from being drafted. One of the guys I had gone through the physical with kept calling me as he was soon to be drafted and sent to boot camp. I never saw him, as we both went our separate ways after the physical; however, I always wondered what happened to guys like that, once we'd met. I soon went to boot camp and was quickly sent to Viet Nam. I always hoped their names were not on the Viet-Nam Memorial in D.C. We landed at Dang but were quickly sent to our base camp. Our base camp was Camp Haines, which was beside the 101st Airborne Camp Eagle, just south of Hue. We were sent all over Viet Nam from there. We worked on the famous Route One to keep the supply route open. We built bridges, installed culverts and headwalls, and also rebuilt and repaired the road on Route 1. We also built bases and camps, LZs (Landing Zones), and firebases. However, we also worked with the Vietnamese on schools, hospitals, and orphanages, many times on our own time. It was terrible to see what the war was doing to Viet Nam. We always hoped we could end the war so the country could get back to normal. We were then moved by LST down the coast and up the river to Saigon. After gathering our supplies, we moved into the iron triangle to build bases for the PBRs (Patrol Boat River). Then our time came for rotation to the states.

CHAPTER 4:
THE SEARCH FOR EMMA

It was a great day, the tropical sun shining, sending its golden rays to light up Bangkok. With the old crumpled paper in my pocket, I headed out of the hotel to find my Thai friend. I waited eagerly for the elevator to come to my floor. Finally, the elevator arrived at my floor and I quickly walked in and pushed the button to take me to the lobby. A Thai man was on the elevator with two nicely dressed Thai ladies when the door opened. After being in Saudi Arabia for so long, the ladies looked exceptional to me. As the elevator stopped and the doors opened, I waited just to watch the ladies walk away.

I slowly walked away from the elevator toward the reception to get a taxi, then changed my plans and decided to eat breakfast before beginning the search for my Thai friend.

I walked to a small table by the window so I could watch what was going on. I slowly sat down and moved to get the best position I could for watching the people around me. I picked up the menu and glanced down it. After not having pork for so long, the ham and eggs on the menu looked like just what I wanted. However, I checked the local breakfast menu and it had rice soup. I never had decisions like that to make at the mess hall in Saudi Arabia. I took the urge to have the long awaited pork and decided to order the ham and eggs. A shy quiet waitress came to me with a glass of water to take my order. Her wide smile and pleasant attitude was just what I needed to start my day.

"Sawaddi, may I take your order" she said as she set the glass of water down in front of me, then did a wai.

"Sawaddi," I answered back, using my language book the best I could.

Her wide smile showed that my attempt at her language pleased her. "May I take your order?" she asked, after passing me the menu.

"I'll have the ham and eggs with the eggs cooked well and a cup of hot tea," I answered her.

"Anything else?" she questioned.

"No, thank you," I responded to her as she noted what I wanted, then she turned and left to get my order.

It was nice to watch the Thai people in their daily routines. Their walking and talking in the tonal Thai language was very strange and different to me. I was totally lost in thought as my breakfast was set before me, which brought me back to the present.

"Anything else I can get for you?" the waitress questioned.

"No, thank you," I responded to her question as I smelled the freshly cooked food. I ate slowly since it had been such a long time since I had any pork. Not being allowed pork just made me want it more. The waitress dropped the bill by as I was finishing my meal. I looked at the bill, which was 42 baht, and I reached in and got a 50 baht bill and left it on the table as I walked out to start the search.

I left the hotel and started down the line of taxis parked at the hotel. Most of them were blue Datsun 4-door sedans. I stopped and started to talk a driver. His English was very good. I pulled out the paper with the directions on it from my shirt pocket and asked the taxi driver if he could take me to the location on the directions. He took the paper and read it carefully.

"Yes," the taxi driver said; he could take me to the location on the paper. "Come get into the taxi and we will go," he responded.

"Wait—what will it cost me?" I asked.

"We can go there for 70 baht," he answered my question. I knew to get a fixed price on the taxi so we would not have to argue later. I climbed into the front seat so that I could see where we were going. However, I got in on the right side, which seemed strange because the Thai are like the British and drive on the left side (wrong side of the road, since we drive on the right side of the road.) of the road.

Thailand is the only country in Asia that was not colonized by the European countries. When the big grab for land was going on in Africa and Asia with all the big European countries, Thailand escaped being colonized. Thailand lost a lot of their land to the European countries, but was able to escape colonization. So their customs are from their own culture, not mixed with a colonial government's culture. The surrounding countries, like Burma, Cambodia, Laos, Viet Nam, and Malaysia, were all colonized. Thailand's flag is red, white, and blue like the US and French flags. Thailand stands alone in not being colonized.

The taxi driver headed out into the mass of cars that made up the traffic. "A lot of traffic now," the taxi driver told me.

I was really glad he spoke and read English so well. I selected him for that reason. "Yes," I agreed with him. "A lot of traffic at this time. Is it always like this?" I asked.

His laugh was really his answer. "More cars than streets in Bangkok, you know," he responded. As we moved through different parts of the city, the driver pointed out different sites and shopping areas and told me about them. Then I told him why I was here: to try to find a Thai man I had met in Viet Nam during the war ten years ago. "Bangkok much changed in ten years; your friend may not live there anymore," he responded.

We were coming to the Victory Monument, which is a traffic circle, and then we took Raichawithi Road. We then took the first road to the left. I counted down seven houses. The seventh house was a new three-story house. We stopped, and I asked the taxi driver if he would come with me, since I did not speak or read Thai. We walked slowly up the stairs to the second floor.

I started to knock on the door when it was opened by a Thai lady. We were really surprised. I tried to speak to her in English, but she could not understand English. The lady was really blazing Thai at me and I could not understand a thing she was saying or meaning, so I turned to the Thai taxi driver for him to explain to me what was going on. He said she was just moving in and I scared her when she opened the door.

Then the driver talked to the people living on the second floor. They did not know Emma Bhamorabutr. They were just moving into the house since it had been remodeled, but did not know who had lived there before. They directed us to an older lady who had lived there longer. She lived next to them, and the lady took us over to her place. They explained to her who I was looking for. She thought about it for a long time, remembering Emma and his family. However, they had moved when he returned from Viet Nam. She did not know where they had moved to—another part of town, or maybe they moved up country. Too much has changed, the lady said; everything was changing.

She provided us a drink of water and Thai tea, which was the custom. We accepted, hoping she would remember something else, but she did not. She told us of someone who may remember, who lived close by. The small Thai apartment was very strange to me. It had pictures of the King, Queen, and of the King's mother. Most had spirit houses that faced all different directions. You could smell that they had been burning incense in the apartments. You could see the picture of some family member who had died and was covered in flowers.

We thanked the lady from the second floor and the old Thai lady for their help and the drinks. With the clasping of hands (the wai) and the traditional Thai greeting, we left. We walked back to the taxi. Two small boys had washed the taxi, and the taxi driver was mad. However, they only wanted 10 baht, so it was easy to end the problem with 10 baht to the boys. The boys clapped their hands and said "Sawaddi" to us. The taxi needed washing, anyway.

We were at a drink stand and I needed something cool to drink. "Would you like to have a cool drink?" I asked the driver. "We have time. I will buy you whatever you want."

We sat at the stools at the pushcart. The operator of the stand asked, "What do you want?"

"What do you have?" I asked.

"We have Pepsi, orange drink, fresh orange juice..." I stopped her then and said I would take the orange juice, as it sounded so good. Then she continued, "—beer..." I quickly answered that instead I would take the beer rather than the orange juice. The taxi driver also agreed that a beer would be better for me.

The old Thai lady brought me a Singha beer and a fresh orange juice for the taxi driver. She set the two drinks in front of us and asked for 50 baht, which I thankfully gave to her. She smiled at us and then it hit me why Thailand is known as "The Land of Smiles". The ice-cold beer really tasted good in the hot climate. I took the label off the beer bottle, showing the "Singha" brand name, and put it in my pocket to save it. This was my first Thai beer in Thailand.

A young girl came by selling necklaces made of flowers that smelled so good. I bought some from the girl, and the taxi driver said the flowers are bought by the Thais for their temples, cars, and houses. "They are to bring you good luck," the taxi driver said. I paid her the 20 baht that she asked for the flowers. The girl clapped her hands in a wai and said "Sawaddi", then hurried along to sell more flowers.

Then an old lady came by and asked to tell my fortune as we were finishing the beers. The taxi driver said "no" to her and she started to leave. Then I said, "Wait a moment; it will just take a minute and we can be on our way." The old Thai lady pulled a stool up beside us and carefully looked at both of my palms. Then she started to speak very slowly.

"You are on a journey and are searching for something that you do not need. You will find something in your journey that you will want, but not what you are searching for."

"What will I find, gold?" I questioned the lady.

"Gold is for fools; they steal and cheat for it to build big houses, but find no happiness," she told me.

"What should I search for then?" I asked her.

"Only you will know what you are searching for and when you have found it," she replied. Then she held out her hand for 10 baht. I gave her the 10 baht for the fortune.

"What could she have meant?" I asked the taxi driver.

"I do not know," he replied. "She is an old fool and her fortune telling is only for fun and leaves more questions than it answers."

I told the taxi driver the last time I had my fortune told was in Viet Nam. I was sitting in a bar beside a nice looking Vietnamese lady, talking to her, when a Vietnamese man came in and asked to tell my fortune.

When I agreed, he took my hand and looked at the palm and then he began.

"You will travel very much all over the world. You will meet many people and have many friends." He told me that I was not married and sadness had filled my heart. "Your sadness will be taken away and you will marry an Oriental woman."

"See," I said, "he was wrong; I have traveled, but I am not married." I set the label-less bottle back on the table, turned to the taxi driver, and said, "Can we go try to find the person who knows Emma, as I have a tour that starts at two o'clock?"

We went back to the much-used little blue Datsun and climbed aboard to head to the next adventure. The driver pulled out into the moving traffic and headed to where the woman had told us to go. The strange sights and sounds made me feel lost in a different world. The little blue Datsun moved like a small boat in an irrigation canal. We turned from the main street and bounced along the side streets to come to a halt in front of group of apartment buildings. We walked to the apartment where the lady told us to go. The door to the apartment was open.

I wondered what I was doing there. I glanced at my watch and it was 11:05AM. A group of people was outside eating lunch. The taxi driver asked them if any of them knew Emma. He said, "The lady from the other apartment told us you may know where he may be." He told them my story, that Emma and I had both been in Viet Nam and had met, and that if either of us was to come to the other's country, we would try to find one another.

The Thai language flowed back and forth between the taxi driver and the people eating lunch at the apartment. Then finally, after a very long conversation, the taxi driver turned to me and said, "They knew Emma a long time ago before they moved and he moved, but now they do not know where he lives." The driver talked to them again, then turned back to me and said, "Since Emma left, there have been many people to come and go; we do not know where you could find Emma."

"Well, what can we do now?" I asked the taxi driver.

"I do not know," he replied.

"Take me back to the hotel—maybe I can think of something later," I told him.

As we walked back to the taxi, I glanced down at my watch and it was almost noon. "Are there any good Thai restaurants near by?" I asked the taxi driver.

"Can you eat Thai food?" the driver answered.

"I can eat anything now, if they have Singha beer," I answered.

"Sure," he replied, "I'll take you; you are going to like it."

The little blue Datsun sprang to life and we headed to another adventure in it. We bounced along in heavy traffic with long stops at the traffic lights, some of which had policemen directing traffic. The Thais are very polite drivers, as they weave in and out of traffic giving people the right of way and getting the right of way from others. Finally, we pulled onto a side street. We came to a stop in front of a brick building with windows all across the front of it. It had a sign on it but it was all in Thai. The driver announced, "This is the place, and you will like the food here."

We walked from the taxi into the restaurant, and I started looking for a place to sit. However, the taxi driver kept walking and walked on through the restaurant and out back onto a patio area covered with a straw roof. He selected a table to sit at and I joined him. As soon as we were seated, a waitress came over with the menu and two glasses of water to our table. She handed each of us a menu. I looked at the menu it was all in Thai.

"I cannot read the menu as it is all in Thai. Bring me a beer and some fried rice, and fried noodles both with pork," I told the driver. The driver spoke to the waitress in

Thai as she did not speak any English and gave her both our orders. She then hurried off to get the orders. Shortly, the waitress returned with a large Singha beer for me and a cup of Thai iced coffee for the taxi driver.

"What will you do this afternoon?" the taxi driver asked.

"I have a tour of the crocodile farm," I answered him.

"I can take you to a really good place tonight, if you want to go and have some fun," the taxi driver said.

I took another drink of the beer. Then I answered him, "Sure, why not?"

"You will really like this place," the taxi driver said. Just then, the waitress appeared with our orders. She set down what we'd ordered in front of us. She asked if there was anything else that we would like. Since the table had plenty of spices and all, we said that we did not need anything now.

A silence fell over the table as we begin to eat our dinner. The Thais have red peppers in fish sauce on the table to flavor your food. I put some on my fried rice as I started to eat it and the driver and the waitress both watched. Suddenly my mouth was filled with fire as I bit down on the small red pepper. I quickly grabbed for the beer and took a drink to put out the fire. I then had my first encounter with the Thai hot peppers. The waitress quickly brought over a banana for me to eat to stop the burning. That is the way the Thais get relief, the driver told me. The hunt for Emma had made me hungry, and I really enjoyed the food. The taxi driver then told me the Thai peppers were very hot, but thought I knew that. Then he added, "The way to stop the burning is to eat a banana."

The food was really good and spicy. We were just finishing eating when I asked the taxi driver, "What time will you pick me up tonight?"

"I will pick you up at eight o'clock in front of the hotel," came his reply.

"Good," I answered. "I will meet you at eight o'clock in front of the hotel." As we finished with lunch, the waitress came over with the bill. It was only 65 baht. I gave her 75 baht. Then we headed back to the little blue Datsun to go back to the hotel.

The traffic was still as crowded as usual when we got back on the main street. The drive back to the hotel was uneventful. The driver pulled up to the front of the hotel, and I paid him an additional 150 baht for all of his help. He reconfirmed that he would be at the hotel at 8:00PM to take me out.

I walked into the hotel and stopped by the reception desk. I took Emma's name and showed it to the girl at the reception desk and she wrote it down. I asked her to check and see if she could find it in the Bangkok phone book. Also, I asked her if she knew any way I could locate Emma. She said she would check the phone book and call to see if he was the one I was looking for. A large part of the Bangkok phone book in my hotel room was in Thai, so I was unable to find Emma in there when I had searched it earlier. I gave her 50 baht to help encourage her search.

Chapter 5: Bangkok Sights

I hurried into the hotel to get my camera, as it was almost time to catch the tour bus. I went up the elevator to my room and got my camera. I picked up a couple of rolls of film just in case I needed them, then glanced at my watch and saw that it was 1:45 as I went back downstairs to the lobby. I got to the lobby just in time to relax for a while.

While I was waiting by the front door of the hotel, up walks Mr. Jim Beam with a girl on each arm. He saw me and came over to me. "I want to thank you for helping me on the plane," he said. "You see, I am afraid of flying, so I get drunk and pass out so I do not have to worry about flying. Do you want to come with us and have some fun?" he asked.

"No, I am catching the tour bus to the crocodile farm here at 2:00," I answered.

"Well, let me buy you a drink," he said, just as the tour bus pulled up in front of the hotel.

"I have to catch my bus; I will take a rain check on the drink. I will see you," I said. The mini bus had already made the rounds of the other hotels, and ours was its last stop before going to the crocodile farm. I climbed aboard the bus and found a seat. Then the bus left for the crocodile farm. The drive was pleasant although the traffic was hectic. The different types of architecture, the new next to the old, made quite a contrast. It was nice to look at it, as the old were so much different from our own buildings.

We arrived at the crocodile farm and left the bus. We were told to look around, and they would announce when the show would start so that we could see it. I wandered around the crocodile breeding tanks and the tanks that had sizes ranging from babies to full-grown crocodiles. I was snapping pictures with my camera and staying with the tour group. We were then escorted to the pit were the show was held. A fairly large crowd had gathered to see the show.

The show was very interesting; the man wrestled the crocodiles had them perform, and the big part was him putting his head in a crocodile's open mouth. He handled the crocodiles very differently than I had seen before. He held his head in the crocodile's mouth, almost daring the crocodile to close it. After the show, we were escorted to the sales room to look at the items made from the crocodile hide. They had wallets, purses, shoes, belts, bags, boots, and a large number of other items. It was interesting, but too early to start buying items on the first day. Since it was almost 6:00, the tour was over. The same group of people crowded back onto the mini bus to return to their hotels. The people were beginning to get tired. The return trip to the hotels was by a different route, so we saw all types of different things. The sun was getting lower on the horizon, which made for some interesting sights.

Being the last on the bus is good, but it also means that you are the last off the bus. I arrived back at the hotel with only enough time to take a shower and change into some different clothes. I stopped by the office to check with the receptionist to see if she had any luck locating Emma in the phone book and by calling. She said, "I made four calls to people with that name but nobody knew Emma." Then she continued, "Many Thais do not have

27

phones, or use somebody else's phone. I hope you can find him. Do you have an address?"

"No," I said. "We never wrote; we only talked and I gave him my address to find me but he only gave me directions to his house, which has changed very much in ten years."

When I opened my room at the hotel, it smelled so good because of the flowers that I had bought earlier. After the shower and a change of clothes, I returned to the lobby. I checked my watch and thought, *Well, I have enough time to walk around on the street to see what is by the hotel.* While I had gone to take a shower, they had also had a rain shower outside. The air smelled so clean and fresh being washed by the rain shower—not like the usual smell of the buses, cars, and garbage. It was pleasant walking and looking in the different shop windows. As I was walking by a tailor shop, I thought I should go in and check on prices to buy some new clothes. I opened the door to the tailor shop and heard the bell ring, announcing my entrance to the tailor shop.

"May I help you?" The man in the shop asked.

"I am looking for a couple of shirts at a really good price," I responded to him.

"Let me show you some that we have, and I know you will like them," he said. Walking to a rack, the man started pulling out different styles of shirts and telling me why I should choose each style. "This is the kind that would look good on you," he suggested.

Pulling a different shirt from the rack, I said, "I like this style; can I try it on?"

"We would be most happy if you would try it on; it will look really good on you," he replied.

I removed my shirt and tried on the shirt I liked; however, it was not large enough to fit me. "It is too small for me; don't you have larger ones?" I asked.

The store made clothes mainly for the Thais and was just starting to get the tourist trade. So most of the clothes they had were made to fit the smaller Thai people. "We can make a shirt just for you, just to fit you," he answered.

"What will it cost to make a shirt to fit me?" I asked.

"About 200 baht, depending on the material you select," he replied.

"Two hundred baht! I can buy shirts for 75 baht," I answered, trying to get him to lower his price. One never pays the asking price in shops like this overseas; if you do, it is really an insult to the people, as they want to barter and get to know their customers. The large stores do have fixed prices, but even at those, one can get reduced prices by buying larger quantities on some items.

"No, I cannot sell it for that cheap price," he replied. "I will let you have it for 150 baht."

"Well, I will tell you what I will do: if you lower your price down to 75 baht, I will take two shirts in this style and two shirts in this other style," I responded to his offer while I continued to look around the shop.

"No, no!" he said. "I must have 150 baht—I cannot go lower than that," came his reply.

I continued to look around the store and he hurried to show me more styles of shirts. Finding the style I wanted and showing them to the operator, I said, "Two shirts of each of these two styles, each for 75 baht."

"No, no! I cannot sell at that low price; I will let you have them for 100 baht each for the four shirts that you want," came his latest offer.

Not getting any better response, I looked around in the little shop some more, then started to leave. "Ok, Ok, I will do for 75 baht each," he said. I agreed to his last offer by nodding my head yes.

Quickly, he took the measurements for my shirts. He wrote the measurements down, but they were in metric, and he soon had all the measurements he needed. The final deal was confirmed. The operator wrote down in English the agreed price on his sales sheet. I was to pay 150 baht then and 150 baht when I picked up the four shirts. I gave him the 150 baht, and he gave me the sales receipt to pick up the shirts. "When will the shirts be ready?" I asked.

"Not tomorrow, but after tomorrow," came his reply.

"I may leave for Pattaya tomorrow," I informed the tailor.

"When you return, you can get the shirts," came his hurried response.

"I will be gone for four days," I answered.

"You can come pick up the shirts when you return from Pattaya; the shirts will be ready for you when you return," he responded.

"Ok," I said. "It's all set; I will pick up the shirts when I get back from Pattaya." I walked back to the hotel with the receipt for the shirts; the weather was so nice, I could really relax.

Chapter 6: A Night Out

The little blue Datsun was sitting outside the hotel waiting like a carriage in the night to carry us out to this evening's new adventure.

I approached the little blue Datsun and taxi driver quickly came to my side of the taxi.

"Are you ready for a night in Bangkok?" the driver asked.

"Yes," I responded, as I opened the door and slid into the blue Datsun. As the driver entered the taxi, I asked. "Where are we going?"

"I have a very special place that you will like," his response came. "All people like you like to go there."

"OK," I answered, as we pulled out into the evening Bangkok traffic. The Bangkok traffic was very heavy at this time of night. We neared an intersection and the traffic lights changed; all of the cars were now subject to the hawkers as they move from stopped car to stopped car, selling their wares. They washed cars, cleaned windows, and sold flowers, newspapers, candy, gum, and even the scented flowers for the temples and shrines. I thought if they did not have something and you asked, they would get it for you. I could not resist buying one of the scented

31

flower wreaths for the temples and shrines. They smelled so good and were threaded by hand with a needle. They were really an art form and smelled so good. I rolled down the car window as the hawker came by selling the wreaths. "Tuliy baht?" I asked, trying to find out how much the wreaths cost and practicing Thai.

"Sip baht," came back the answer in correct Thai. I handed her 20 baht and held up two fingers as she sold two of the wreaths to me. I handed one to the taxi driver and he quickly placed it around the rear view mirror. I kept the second one for myself. Just then, the light changed, and the hawkers hurried to the sidewalk to keep from becoming a bump in the road as the traffic threatened to roll over them.

Bangkok is a pretty town at night. I enjoyed the night sounds and sights, all very new to me being a first time visitor to Bangkok. I thought how lucky I was to be able to enjoy things like this, to be able to add Thailand to my list of countries where I have been. I have been to all the six major continents: North and South America, Europe, Asia, Africa, and Australia.

Twisting and turning, the taxi worked its way down the busy streets past the ever present and busy crowds that were walking down the streets, catching buses, and, most of all, eating at the little push carts that sell all of the Thai noodles and foods. Turning off the main street, we went a short distance and made another turn. Then we pulled in to what looked like a hotel. It was a large "L" shaped building, with three stories. The rectangle lot was mostly filled by the L-shaped building, of which the longer part ran along the long leg of the rectangle lot and the short leg the short side of the rectangle. The driver found a parking place for the little blue Datsun.

We both got out and walked to the large double doors that must have been the entrance to the hotel; however, I could not see any sign like on the other hotels. The place was not very well lit, either. When neared the door, there was hardly any noise. Expecting a hotel with a band, I thought they must be on break since it was so quiet. When we approached the door, the doorman appeared and opened the door for us. We entered into a mostly darkened room. It took a short time for my eyes to adjust to the dimly lit room. We were hustled to a table and were seated. The waiter asked what we wanted to drink. I requested a Singha beer; the taxi driver ordered, and the waiter left. My mind was wandering, thinking about meeting Emma so long ago, the things we had seen in Viet Nam, and my work in Saudi Arabia.

We were sitting in a room with twelve to fifteen tables. People were seated at about eight or ten of them. At that time, a girl returned with the drinks. My mind was still occupied with the past. At the front of the room was a large glass window, which separated another room from the room in which we were seated. The room had a color television set by the glass window. In front of the color television set were four rows of bleachers, on which sat all shapes and sizes of Thai girls watching the television set. Each girl wore a pin with a number on it on her right side, by her right arm. They were dressed in all different ways from slacks and blouses to party and evening gowns.

Just as I started to talk to the taxi driver, a group of people got up and walked out of the room to go outside. An older lady got up from the table where they were sitting and came toward the table where we were. With the lights shining down on the girls, they were unable to see who was sitting at the tables in front of them. "What is happening here?" I asked the taxi driver.

"Girls," he responded. "I brought you here because you did not have a girl and you looked so lonely. Here you can get yourself a lovely girl." He continued, "All you have to do is pick out the girl you like that is seated in front of us. Then she will come out here to meet you and you can go with her."

At that time, the older lady arrived at our table with her drink. She sat at our table and did not say anything for a short while. The table seemed uncomfortably silent before she broke it by saying, "We have so many lovely young Thai girls to go with you, which one will you choose?"

"I, uh...I, uh...I want the girl to choose," I answered. "I mean, I want the girl to come with me because she wants to, not because she is paid to," I responded.

Again the lady spoke, "With all of these girls and you want to waste your time trying to get some girl outside or out of some bar?"

How easy, I thought, *all you have to do is make a selection, pay your money, and you have a girl.*

"How long will you be staying in Bangkok?" the lady asked.

I could feel the business side in her prompting her part of the conversation to get what she needed to know. "I leave for Pattaya tomorrow," I answered, hoping to get out of the position that I was put in, as I was not really going there that early. I hoped my leaving tomorrow would end the awkward position in which I'd been placed.

"Oh, good, then the girl can go with you to Pattaya," the lady responded. She turned to the waitress and spoke Thai to her, and the waitress hurried off. "The girls like to go to Pattaya," the lady said. Expecting another drink from the lady's instructions to the waitress, I finished my beer as she continued. "You can take any girl; if you don't like her, you can bring her back and take another girl." This lady knew all the answers and had me on the ropes. "Since this is your first time in Bangkok, I will give you a special deal." Now she started on the hard sell. "You take the girl for seven days, and you pay only for five days."

I was just about to respond to her when I felt a soft hand brush through my hair and turned to see a cute Thai girl in slacks and a very nice blouse, smiling at me. The perfume she was wearing caught my senses. "Hi, handsome, I like you." Her Thai-English was as cute as she was as she slid into a chair beside me at the table where we were sitting. It had been so long since I had been close to any girl, it was like finding an oasis in the desert. "Oh, we can do lots of things, and I like to go to Pattaya." She smiled and continued, "I can show you many things in Pattaya."

Another beer was placed in front of me as the lady brought more pressure on me. "I know you will like Ty; she is one of our best girls and she knows all about Pattaya, and can get you many bargains at the shops," the lady informed me. "She can save you her price at the bargains she will get you in Bangkok." The girl patted my knee as I was trying to drink my beer and to keep from thinking about how long it had been since I was out with a lady.

"No, no, no…I just cannot do that," I said. The people at all the tables looked at me like I was crazy. Ty got up and ran out as I was trying to explain to the taxi driver what I was looking for, just a place to dance, drink a beer or two, then go back to the hotel. However, before that I could finish my sentence, the older lady started again. "You no like Ty, no problem, I get you another lady." As her arm went up, I tried to explain what I wanted.

"Look, I am used to going and meeting a girl at a dance or some place and having dinner and all. This just isn't my way," I responded.

"Oh, you waste too much money that way," the lady responded; as she continued, two hands came around my neck from a lady behind me I could not see. Her hands ran over my face as her breast pushed against the back of my head. The woman's soft skin (that I had not felt for so long a time) was again very, very tempting, with the sweet smelling perfume. I turned quickly to get a kiss on my forehead, as a really lovely Thai lady in a flowered summer dress appeared before me.

"This is a special lady," the old Thai lady continued, with her very hard sell amid my shrinking commitment to do things my way. "I know you will like

35

her, she my very best lady. Don't you like her?" the old lady continued.

Gee, I was thinking, this lady could sell ice to Eskimos or run for president and get elected, or even sell the Golden Gate Bridge. She was impossible to say no to!

The girl was about five foot, three inches tall, with long black hair that seemed to flow like water in a mountain stream as she walked. The smile she had would light the way for anybody. She had the look of an actress, the shape to fill out a swimming suit in all of the right places. "How about it, are you taking me to Pattaya?" she questioned as her dark eyes sparkled in the dimly lit room.

"Look, you are a very lovely girl and you look just wonderful, even more than wonderful – you're beautiful or something. But…it is just not my way," I said, knowing I had to escape this place as soon as possible.

"How can you make so lovely of a lady so sad?" the old Thai lady who had all of the answers asked.

Knowing if I stayed, they could win me over, I got up, threw 200 baht on the table to cover the drinks and headed for the door. The taxi driver rushed after me. "You will be back" the old Thai lady shouted after me as I went through the door. I walked past the doorman and outside and finally reached the taxi with the taxi driver just behind me. He started to speak. "What wrong, boss? You no like the girls here? They very pretty, don't you think?"

"Look!" I said very angrily. "You understand, when I get a girl I want her to come with me because she wants to, not because she is paid to. Can you understand that?"

"No, no, you waste time and money. You go back, the girls are very lovely, no waste time. If you no like, you take back, get different one, it save you time, money, and you have much fun." The driver was saying as I climbed in the taxi. He got in also, after a short time waiting for me to change my mind. After a time, he said, "I know, will take you to Pat Pong street, you will like it there." He started the little blue Datsun and left the parking lot, heading for a new adventure.

The little blue Datsun moved out into the crowded night traffic of Bangkok. We weaved our way through the long line of cars and headed toward a different area of town. I was really glad to get out of the brothel that we were in, but *damn*, the ladies really looked so good and smelled so good and spoke English. Well, I had made my first mistake in where to go in Bangkok.

The little blue Datsun was pulling into a parking place. The taxi driver said with a confident smile, "You will like this." We got out of the taxi and I followed the taxi driver to a well-lit area with a lot of loud music. This was the opposite from where we had just come. It was a quiet, dimly lit area with passion as the major item for sale. We moved down the street and the driver disappeared in a club and I walked by to check it out. I paused to check out the outside of the club, and just as I did, I felt a pat on my butt. Turning, I came face to face with a young lady who had on an outfit that left very little to the imagination.

Before I could gain my senses, she said, "Come on in, honey, we can have some drinks and dance and just have some fun."

"I was just going in" I said. Then I stepped aside to let her go first. As I entered, I looked around to see where the taxi driver had gone. Not finding him, I started for a corner table. Then the girl grabbed my arm and led me to a table where two other girls were sitting. "This is Molly," she indicated, pointing to a girl dressed about like her, only with a different color outfit. "This is Susan," as she pointed to a girl in a very *mini* mini-skirt with a skimpy blouse. The mini-skirt was almost just a wrap-around band of cloth. "I am Dawn." Sitting down, she pulled me down with her. "Now, what's your name, what are you drinking, and where you from?" she said. Not waiting for an answer, she called over the waitress to order drinks.

"Well, I am Ed. I am from the States, and I would like to order a Singha." I finally got out something. A quick signal from Dawn and the waitress turned before she reached the table and hurried away. Before I could understand what was happening, the waitress returned with four drinks and placed them in front of everybody, as she must have done hundreds of times. The beer tasted really good, the music was too loud, and the room was full of smoke. The smoke created different layers in the room from almost the floor to the ceiling, making me choke for breath.

"Well, what are you going to do tonight, honey?" Dawn asked.

"I am just out for a little while to see the sights," I replied.

"Well, we can sure have some fun," Dawn said. She finished her drink and signaled the waitress for another round. These girls were so fast, they could make the Indy 500 look like a wheelbarrow race. "Lets dance," Dawn said.

"Oh, alright," I answered.

Off we went to the tiny, overcrowded dance floor. The band was small and really loud. I could not even remember the songs that were played and sung. We stayed on the dance floor for three songs, then headed back to the table. There were already three guys sitting at the table when we returned from dancing, and no empty chairs. Using that as good reason to look for the taxi driver, and to get out of all the smoke, which was beginning to get to me, I left saying "I have to find my taxi driver." Dawn was already circling her next prey and did not even notice me leaving.

The smoke was causing tears to come to my eyes as I was looking for the driver, so I stepped outside. I had hardly cleared the door when another girl swept me away into another bar; a couple of drinks and a few dances later, I was back on the sidewalk trying again to get smoke out of my eyes. Just then, I was lucky enough to find the taxi driver. "Let's go someplace that is not so noisy and not so much smoke." I said to him.

"You no like girls?" came the reply from the taxi driver.

"Yes! I like girls – I am not a queer!" I replied in a very hard voice.

"We try one more place," the taxi driver said "You like it, it's called Thai Heaven."

The cool outside air felt good clearing the smoke from my eyes. We walked past the bars, on the way to the taxi. The girls used their most persuasive gestures to get us to come back into the bars.

The little blue Datsun sat waiting for us to come back and continue our night out in Bangkok. I climbed in and it felt so good just to sit down. I had not realized how tired I was until I we sat down. The little blue Datsun came to life as we moved out into the nighttime traffic of Bangkok. We headed along, turning here and turning there. We came to a main street, and in a short time, we were in front of the club and the taxi driver pulled up to the front door and stopped. The doorman opened my car door and I slid out. The taxi left since I had already agreed to the amount I owed him and had paid him.

"Good evening, sir; welcome to Thai Heaven," the doorman said while opening the door for me to enter.

"Thank you," I said, as I walked through the door he had opened for me. As I entered, a waitress took me to a table with a flashlight, where I sat down. It was dark and cool inside, with hardly any smoke. "What would you like to drink?" the waitress asked.

"Give me a Singha," I answered.

Just at that time, the song that everybody was doing the bump to in those days was playing. It sure was a change from the last place I'd been. The waitress brought my beer, and I asked her where the restrooms were. She pointed in the direction of the restroom, then I got up and worked my way toward the restroom.

The place was mostly dark except the dance floor, which was dimly lit. The bathrooms always had a person to hand out a towel to you when you got to the sink. Geckos were also always around in the bathroom, running on the walls and ceilings, catching the bugs that found their way through the screens. They were so famous, they had shirts and carvings of them.

When I returned to my table, the song was just ending, and two girls who were dancing together returned to the table next to mine. They were good at dancing, but it looked strange to me for the two girls to be dancing. As the next song started, I asked one of the girls if she wanted to dance.

"Sure", she said, and off to the dance floor we went.

It sure seemed strange and wonderful to be dancing and holding a girl again. The song ended and the lights came on, as they announced they were going to have the Thai boxing bout. Carpets were rolled out and a small ring was set up for the bout. Thai boxing is different from normal boxing, as the Thais can also use their legs and feet. This was long before these bouts became popular in the U.S. Both girls moved to my table and were explaining to me what was happening. The two Thai boxers were brought in and introduced. They went through a routine to honor the trainer, Buddha, and others before they started the fight. All this time, I was talking to the two girls. They suggested we bet on the fighters. One fighter was in red and one was in blue. Since I thought the bigger fighter would win, I bet on the bigger one in blue. The bet was for a noodle dinner after the show.

The fight was ready to start, and the two Thai boxers were brought out to the center of the ring and touched gloves. They returned to their corners, the bell rang, and the fight started. Thai music was played on a flute as the boxers fought. The larger boxer in blue quickly struck the right side of the head of the other smaller boxer. He went wheeling across the ring to the ropes on the other side. As the bigger boxer moved in, a quick kick to the side of the head by the little boxer sent the bigger boxer wheeling to the ropes. Then a quick kick to the ribs kept the bigger boxer off balance as the smaller boxer moved into position to cause more damage.

The bigger boxer hung onto the ropes as the referee moved in to separate the boxers and get them off the ropes. The fight continued. The bigger fighter may have been stronger, but the smaller fighter could take the punishment and was quicker than the larger fighter. Every time the large fighter struck, the smaller fighter managed to ward off the attack and land more punches and kicks on the larger fighter, giving him more than he could handle.

In the middle of an attack on the large fighter, the bell rang, sending both fighters to their corners. Since this fight was only to show how Thai boxing works, the referee selected the small boxer in red shorts as the winner of that night's fight. Then everybody threw Thai baht notes into the ring for both fighters. It was an interesting show with the blow-by-blow description being given by the two Thai ladies.

Quickly, the ring was cleared from the dance floor. However, before the dance could start again, a group of Thai ladies dressed in classical Thai costumes came onto the dance floor. The announcer announced that they will perform a classical Thai dance. The musicians came in and set up their classical Thai instruments and started playing. The Thai dancers started dancing to the music, with their slowly moving bodies moving with the precision of a well oiled machine. The long fingernails swayed as the bodies swung gracefully to the music. The outfits were of Thai silk, made famous in the United States by Jim Thompson, who was a OSS officer during WWII in Asia who stayed in Thailand to start the Oriental Hotel, then the export of Thai silk to the U.S. before he disappeared mysteriously.

The ladies in their very colorful Thai outfits seemed out of place in this place, but they were very exotic and wonderful to watch. The dancers' slow and careful movements and costumes acted out an important part of the Thai culture. The long fingernails on the extended hands showed the lack of work done by the original dancers in that period. They must have been true artisans in the old days. The graceful dance was over too quickly and the dancers and the musicians left the floor.

The band started to play again and I asked the taller girl to dance. It was a slow song and it was also getting late. When we got on the floor, the girl said, "My name is Lee. Please ask Thumb to dance."

I had not thought how the talk at the table was mostly between Lee and me, and Thumb must have felt left out. I said, "The next dance I will dance with Thumb." It was nice to see how thoughtful Lee was about Thumb. The song came to an end, and before we could sit down, the band had started with another song. I leaned over and asked Thumb if she wanted to dance. She was up in a flash. She was a lot smaller than me, and she was really talkative. Thumb said, almost without stopping for any answer, "Are you American? Is this your first time to Thailand? How do you like Thailand? How do you like Thai food?"

I finally broke in rudely to answer her questions before she could ask a lot more questions, replying, "Yes, I am from America, and this is my first trip to Thailand. Yes, I like Thailand – it has many different customs from America – and yes, I like the Thai food I have tried."

Thumb continued with her rapid questions and speech. "Don't forget you owe us a noodle dinner after the show. I think we should go before the noodle carts get too crowded, because this place and the other places close at midnight, and if we get there early, we won't have to wait so long." With only a quick pause and before I could speak, she continued, "I know a really good place to get noodles; I think you would like that since it is a really good place."

The song ended, and we walked over to the table. As we sat down, Thumb continued her rapid-fire speech. "I think we should finish our drinks and go get some noodles, we can get there before the rest of the crowd leaves the clubs at midnight."

I was just finishing my beer as the girls were finishing their drinks, giving me a chance to speak. "Yes, now would be a good time to leave and beat the crowd to the noodle shops, don't you think?" Both girls nodded as they placed their glasses on the table.

Thumb led the way to the door, with Lee right behind her and me bringing up the rear. Out the door we went, and Thumb was already flagging down a taxi as I cleared the door. We all piled into the taxi and headed to their favorite noodle stand. The sky was clear now and so full of stars. Traffic was clearing out some, so there was not the long wait at the lights. We pulled up to an area where there were lots of carts and noodle vendors.

As we stopped, the vendor hurried to add stools for us at a small table. The taxi driver joined us as we sat down at the table. Thumb was still talking as she had been since we left Thai Heaven, and was already ordering as we were sitting down. Everybody else ordered and questioned me as to what I wanted. They said they had ordered me a bowl of noodles with pork. They asked what I wanted to drink. I told them one more beer. The vendor did not have beer but hurried to another stand to get it for me. She returned with it and with the drinks for the others. She hurried to bring each of us the bowls of noodles we had ordered. As if almost by magic, the little lady who ran the stall produced a fork for my noodles while the others ate with chopsticks. Thumb had the capability to continue talking while she ate her noodles. Not that she really said anything – just that she made a lot of noise while she ate her noodles.

It was nice to sit in the open and not have the crowd and the cigarette smoke surrounding me. "Gee!" I said "I had almost forgotten about tomorrow – I have to go to the floating market. I have to leave the hotel at 7:00AM, I think." I paid for the noodles and Thumb stayed, finishing her noodles and still talking, as Lee, the taxi driver, and I left for my hotel. The taxi driver dropped us at the hotel; it had been a long day for me, and Lee and I headed for the room. We both went to bed and were soon fast asleep.

The telephone rang as I had just finished shaving. It was Thumb, still talking; she was waiting for us at the restaurant downstairs for breakfast. I told her that Lee was not ready yet, but we would be right down.

Lee told me Thumb would know what to order for her for breakfast. She told me to go on and order and she would be right down. I left for the restaurant as Lee headed for the bathroom. Thumb was waiting for me as I got off the elevator, and she was still talking about something, I really was not listening to her to find out what she was talking about. The Thais never stopped amazing me; Thumb was nice, neat, and clean, with the smell of a fresh flower. Even though the Thais have no bathrooms as the Americans have. We went into the restaurant, found a table, and were seated. We sat next to a table occupied by two American couples. The two ladies looked like they had just came from a two-week march and smelled as bad. They had on sweatshirts that did not look like they had been cleaned since they bought them. What was really a shame was that they were sitting by some nice, neat lady from Thailand.

Soon, the waitress came to our table and took our three orders and hurried off to place them. Thumb continued her talk about something. Then, just as our orders came, Lee came to our table. Lee was neat and looked good in a blue silk top and matching slacks. My breakfast was American, with ham, two eggs, toast, and a cup of tea. The girls had rice soup and toast, which a lot of the Thais eat for breakfast, with orange juice. Thumb continued talking throughout the meal.

People were gathering in the lobby for the tour as we were finishing our breakfast. We had time to make the tour, as the bus had not yet arrived when we joined the others waiting. The bus arrived and the tour operator came in to get us. We all boarded the bus and headed toward the floating market. It has always been nice to travel through different countries and see different building styles; it has always amazed me.

The tour bus pulled up to the dock area. Everybody left the bus and traded their bus seat for seats on the Thai riverboat. It was long and narrow, like a dugout canoe; however, the power was furnished by a regular 4- or 6-cylinder car engine. It was mounted on a swivel with a long drive shaft that went out behind the boat with a prop. To move, they let the front of the engine go up, which lowered the drive shaft with the prop in the back into the water, and it surged forward at a fast rate. The Orientals always come up with whatever they need to get the job done. The last time I saw something like that was in Viet Nam, but they were using a discarded one cylinder engine to power that boat and it was six miles out to sea where one could not see land. A family lived on that boat.

As we moved along the river (the Klong actually was a hand dug canal), we stopped to buy fruit from the people selling along the Klong. The Thais had some of the best fruit in the world, I discovered, and it was best when it was fresh. They had a red colored fruit that had thorns coming out of it, but they were not hard thorns. It was called look nock; when the outer shell was peeled off, it looked like a giant grape and was really delicious. They had a purple colored fruit they called mankoat; when the outer purple layer was peeled off, it was snow white inside and tasted so great, it seemed to just melt in my mouth. Alternatively, they had a fruit called tulian that smell like a toilet, but they said it was really good to eat. (The Thais called these fruits by these names to us; however, they also had proper Thai names for them.)

The houses were built right on the river, with their porches extending out into the river. They did their washing and took their baths on these porches. The people seemed so busy and happy. Their clothes seemed so different from the American style. They were quite friendly to us as the large boat made its way through their "front yards" in the river. Cameras stayed busy as everybody on the tour was snapping pictures of the foreign river lifestyle. Thumb continued her talking, as usual. I wondered if she also talked in her sleep. She was a nice looking lady, but she never shut up.

The boat pulled up to a market that was right on the river. Everybody climbed out to look at the items displayed in the shops.

The girls went to look at some shirts. I wandered around and picked up some post cards that I should have written and mailed out already. I picked up a few souvenirs, getting a spoon for my mother with Thailand written on it, as she collects them. I'd sent her spoons from a lot of different countries. I saw a set of bronze ware, which was really different. The girls came back with the things they had picked out. We went to pay for our purchases before the boat left. It was time to board the Thai boat, or water taxi as some call them. The ride back was interesting, as we passed the Temple of Dawn and saw a lot of other sights. The ride ended all too quickly for me. We came to the dock, and it was time to unload and get back on the bus.

We all got back on the bus for the stops at the different hotels. On the way back, we went through the old Chinese section . This was still where a lot of the Thais went to trade and buy new gold. They had gold shops that are just unbelievable. The Thais sold small gold chains made like small bars of gold with a loop at each end that connected to the other one just like it. They valued the weight of the chains using baht, and a two baht chain was the same as one ounce of gold. Gold was a very important part of the older Thai security system, in which they bought gold when they had money to save, and sold it when they had a need to buy something. Like the Navajo Indians, who used silver, and some who used seashells or other stones, etc. It was unbelievable how a system that started so long ago was used and still worked in modern times.

The bus came to a halt at our hotel, and we got off and put our packages in the hotel room. We talked about where we would go for lunch. We went back to the lobby and hurried to find a taxi to go to lunch at the Thai restaurant, because the noon hour traffic was just unbelievable. One could never believe it unless they had experienced it.

We arrived at the Thai restaurant, and Thumb was still talking. *How can she manage to talk so much and say so little? Maybe she should be a politician,* I thought. Politicians and lawyers were the only people I knew who could talk like that and never say anything.

At least it was cool as we were ushered to a nice table by the window. We could see both the action on the street as well as the action in the restaurant. The waiter came and asked what we wanted to drink. I said a Singha and the girls ordered orange drinks. Also, the girls ordered the typical Thai food. I ordered a Thai meat salad and fried noodles with prawns. Both were really good, and the meat salad was really spicy, which went well with the Singha – it was the only way to eat it. The meal was excellent. It was time to return back to the hotel to catch the tour bus and go to the Rose Garden. I was glad we were not far from the hotel since, even with all of the traffic, we made it back in plenty of time for the next tour.

When the tour bus came to the hotel, we all got aboard and it was off to the Rose Garden. Thumb continued the endless talking like somebody was listening to her. The bus ride to the Rose Garden was long, and we passed a lot of really nice temples in different parts of the city. The Rose Garden was in a large garden area with fishponds and picnic areas at the edge of the city. The bus unloaded, and the people wandered around the different booth areas. They had pythons and monkeys with which one could get a picture taken, or one could take a ride on an elephant. They had all kinds of Thai craft items for sale at the booths.

The bells sounded and we were taken to a large tent arena for the show. The Thais have a really interesting history, and it was acted out in the arena. They used whatever tools they could in the battles they fought. One of the things they had was the elephant. They showed how elephants were used in battle, how the Thais fought with two swords or with one sword and a shield, and also how spears were used, in addition to other weapons used in fighting. They even held a Thai wedding ceremony. Then the show concluded with the classical Thai dancing, and people from the crowd were encouraged to join into the dancing at the end of the show. With the show over, we went back to the bus for the ride back to the hotel. It had been a nice day and we went a different way back, seeing different parts of the city and stopping at all the other hotels first since ours was the last stop. Thumb was still talking as we got back to the hotel.

We went to the hotel room to take a shower and get cleaned up. We were trying to decide where we should go for supper. We all agreed to try out a Mexican restaurant. We went down to the lobby and walked down the street to find a taxi. We found a taxi and agreed on a price before we left for the restaurant. Most of the taxis had meters, but they did not work, so it was always a good idea to agree on the fare before getting into the taxi so there would be no argument at the end of the taxi ride. We arrived at the Mexican restaurant in the rush of the Bangkok traffic. The doorman at the restaurant was a midget. He was dressed up like a real doorman, and since a lot of people were taking his picture, I was sure he helped to bring in customers to the restaurant. The doorman opened the door to the restaurant for us and we went in. It was decorated with Mexican scenes, with sombreros, guitars, blankets, and other items hung on the wall. The waitress, dressed in a Mexican dress, came over to us and escorted us to a table. Leaving us a menu, she took our drink orders and left to go get the drinks. We all looked at the menu and decided to get the special, which was a mixture of Mexican food, Spanish rice, refried beans, tacos, burritos, and similar fare. The waitress returned with our drinks and took our orders and left to get them placed.

We had some quiet time to talk about the day as we sipped our drinks and rested, waiting for the orders to be brought to our table. It was nice, as we had been really rushed all day to see everything and make all the tours. Our orders came to the table steaming hot on hot plates. The food was really good for a place 10,000 miles from where it originated. As we were finishing our food, we were trying to decide where we would go that night. Finally, we agreed to go back to Thai Heaven. After finishing the meal, I paid and went out the door, which was opened by the midget doorman. After handing him a tip, he got a taxi for us. Once we agreed on a price, we headed back to Thai Heaven.

We got to Thai Heaven between 9:30 and 9:45. It was the start of a nice night. I was glad I did not have to go through what I went through night before. The band was different and was even better, or maybe I was just in a better mood. The shows seemed even better than the previous night. We bet on the fighters again – different ones – but this time I was lucky enough to select the winning fighter. We danced and talked a lot, closing down Thai Heaven, then made the journey to the noodle shops. Still Thumb was talking. It was nice when Lee and I were dancing, because I did not have to listen to Thumb talk. We left Thumb talking at the noodle stand as Lee and I headed for the hotel.

Chapter 7: Pattaya

I was up and packed before Lee woke up. Today was the trip to Pattaya. It would be nice to feel the salt water again. Just at that moment, the phone rang. It was Thumb, who was in the lobby and waiting to eat breakfast with us. Lee woke up just in time for me to hand the phone to her. Then a long exchange in Thai started. I decided not to wait for the conversation to end. I told Lee I would meet her downstairs and left for the elevator. The elevator ride was quick and when the door opened, I was in the lobby. I looked for Thumb, but she must have still been on the phone. I waited a while to see if I could find Thumb, but, not seeing her, I went to the restaurant.

When I reached the restaurant, a waitress came to seat me and offered me a seat at the bar. I showed her three fingers and said there will be three of us, and she took me to a table. I could hear Thumb talking to someone as she was headed for the table where I was sitting. She did not seem to miss a beat and was talking to me before reaching the table, and continued talking as she sat down. I managed to get Thumb to stop talking long enough to tell her, "I am leaving for Pattaya today".

"Is Lee going with you?" she asked.

"No," was my reply.

"Do you want me to go with you?" Thumb said, never missing an opportunity.

"No," I said "I need to be alone for a while; I am going to look at the boats they build there and do some scuba diving," I told her.

The waitress came over and took our orders. I decided to try the Thai breakfast of rice soup along with the girls this morning. The waitress was bringing the tea and orange juice to our table as Lee arrived.

Thumb continued her talking with me not really listening to her, but I would nod my head as if I was listening. Just then, the waitress brought us our breakfast. The soup was better than I had thought. It made a nice breakfast, but I would not want it all the time like the Thais eat it.

"Lee," Thumb said, "Ed is going to Pattaya today!" Then came a strange silence for a while; even Thumb did not say anything. I had talked to Lee about this before.

"Lee, I need to be alone and go fishing, diving, snorkeling, and look at the boats that are built near Pattaya," I said.

"Ed," Lee spoke to me to try to get me to change my mind. "I like fishing and I have never tried diving and would like to go."

"Lee," I said, "we would not be together when I am off doing these things and it would be lonely for you. We have had some really good times, and when I come back, we can have some more." As we finished breakfast, there was a kind of uneasy feeling. After breakfast, we left Thumb and went back to the room. Lee picked up her things from the room. I sorted through my bag; I had bought a necklace for Lee that she did not know about and gave it to her. She seemed surprised and happy. She had picked it out on the floating market and had put it back, telling me it was too expensive. Also in the package was some money for her to buy what she wanted. She managed a big smile and gave me a really big kiss. We talked about when I would return from Pattaya and agreed I could find her at Thai Heaven.

Just at that moment, the phone rang. I picked up the phone and it was the lobby. The taxi to take me to my hotel at Pattaya was waiting for me. I picked up my bag and waited for Lee so we could leave together. We made our way to the elevator and got on and pushed the button to take us to the lobby. When we reached the lobby, Thumb was there still talking and not saying anything. I could see the taxi driver waiting for me by the door. The three of us walked out the door followed by the taxi driver. The taxi driver opened the trunk, and I put in my bag. I hugged and kissed Lee and Thumb goodbye and climbed into the taxi.

Traffic was really bad as I left the hotel. *If only Bangkok could improve on the traffic*, I thought, but guessed it was the same in every major city. We headed out of Bangkok a different way. It was nice to see different sights. Leaving the city, there were several seafood restaurants. We crossed several rivers or klongs, I could not tell which. Then we crossed the major river, which had all of the rice barges on it. Some were full going down the river and some were empty or almost empty going back up the river. We passed stalls of people selling crabs with their claws tied and stacked on shelves like one would find canned goods in a grocery store.

We came to an area where rice fields could be seen in all directions. Each side of the highway had rice fields bordering it. We could see the farmers in the fields with their water buffaloes working, plowing or some other activity. Then we came to a field with a lot of women and men planting rice. The fields were flooded, and the people were up to their knees in water, bending over with the bundle of rice sprouts they were planting, one sprout at a time. We came to a wind water pump that was taking water from the canal and emptying it into the rice field. What a wonderful sight – no wasted energy there. We came to a field where a man had a motor powered tractor that he walked behind – some new technology. We passed a field with both the tractor and the water buffalo working together. We saw some of the new diesel powered water pumps that were pumping the water from the canals into the rice fields.

As we left the rice fields, we entered a hilly area. It had several Chinese cemeteries on the outskirts of the town. There was a large Buddhist Temple on the tallest hill or mountain that I could see. It was really nice and could be seen from a long distance. Since it was after 12:00, I asked the driver if we could stop some place for lunch.

The driver pulled off the road and stopped at a restaurant. It had all kinds of pictures on the menu, but all the writing was in Thai. It had a picture of a hamburger, and I confirmed with the driver that it *was* actually a picture of a hamburger before ordering it. It had been a long time since I had had a good hamburger. The Thai taxi driver ordered some noodles. We talked while we were waiting on the orders. I asked the driver how long it took to drive to Pattaya. He scratched his head and thought a while, then said, "It takes about four hours because we have so much traffic and the roads not too good."

We got our food and the hamburger, which really *tasted* like a hamburger – I was really surprised. We finished our meal and returned to the taxi to finish the trip.

We passed over a hill and I could see the waves of the blue sea in front of us. The driver said that Pattaya was still a long way off. We continued down the road to Pattaya with me expecting to see it at any minute. Finally, we crossed over a hill and I could see the sea a short distance off. We rounded a big curve and headed down a twisted road that had tropical trees on each side – some coconut trees, some banana trees, and some I did not know. Finally, we made a big turn and we were driving along the beach. We continued driving, passing houses and small stores. We came to an area where it only had a building on the roadside away from the beach. We continued driving and soon there were stores, shops, and restaurants on both sides of the road and even on piers out into the sea. We continued until the road ended at a hotel on the end of the beach. The driver stopped and said, "This is your hotel."

We got out of the taxi and the driver opened the trunk to get my bag. We were at the Bayshore Hotel. The bellman took my bag as I went to the reception desk to check in, followed by the taxi driver. The taxi driver got his ticket signed to confirm that I made it to the hotel. By the time I got my room assigned, it was already after 3:00. The porter took me to my room, which was on the third floor, and I gave him a tip for bringing my bag, then he left me in my room. I went to the window and looked out, and it was really beautiful, with the clear blue sky meeting the rolling waves of the sea. I unpacked my underwater camera that I had gotten in Toronto, Canada, while I was waiting to get my Saudi visa. Now I would get a chance to use it.

I was in Pattaya, finally. My vacation days were clicking off rather quickly.

Since the hotel had a really nice pool, I decided to use it. I changed into my swimming suit and headed down to the pool. I wanted to take just a quick dip in the pool to get back my water wings a little bit before I went to find something for supper. The water was so blue and nice. I dived in and swam from one end to another. Finally, I got out to rest. There was a bar at the pool so I could have a Singha while I lay down on the lounge to relax. It was just a good time to enjoy being alive. There was a nice stretch of beach in front of the hotel. However, it was starting to get dark already, so I went back to the room to take a shower. I really felt good after a nice shower; however, I was getting hungry. I thought I would walk down on the strip and see what I could find to eat.

They had a lot of restaurants operated by American and Europeans. The quiet little strip really came to life when it turned dark. All the lights on the strip lighted the way, and the people were trying to get me into the clubs to dance and drink. I found a nice little restaurant run by an American and went in to see what they had. A cute waitress brought me a menu and I ordered a Singha till I could find out what I wanted on the menu. Pork chops were on the menu and they came with vegetables and fries. Boy, did that sound good to me! The waitress returned, and I gave her my order as she set the Singha down in front of me. She wandered off to get my order, as I sat on the porch and enjoyed watching and listening to the crowds going by.

They had a really different taxi there, which were very small pickups that had a cover over the back and a cut out behind the driver's seat in the wall of the pickup bed for access to the two seats in the bed. It was the only place I had seen this. Since the strip was not very long, the bed seats in the pickups made it easy for people to get in and out for short distance travel.

My pork chops arrived, and I continued to watch the crowd as I ate. It had been a long time since I had had pork chops and they tasted really good. When I finished supper and paid, the waitress brought me a paper that showed their breakfast menu. I stuck it in my pocket and headed on down the strip, just realizing how tired I was after eating.

Anchored on the strip of beach without bars and shops was a fleet of Thai fishing boats. I made my way to them and started talking to the owners about going out the next day. A lot of them were already rented. However, I found one that was not. I bargained with the owner, who slept on the boat, for a trip the next day. We finally agreed on going out fishing in the morning, then going to the island in the afternoon so I could snorkel around the coral on the island and take pictures. We were to leave at 6:00AM the following morning. I paid him half of the agreed fare and would pay the remaining before leaving in the morning. I had started walking back to the hotel when I passed a place that had dive trips. I talked to an operator who said they were doing check out dives at the local swimming pool the day after tomorrow. If I were to come by the dive shop after the boat trip tomorrow, I could get everything set up with the owner. He gave me a card with a phone number to call if I needed to contact them later. It was late and I was tired and needed to get up early, so I walked back to the hotel. Reaching the hotel, I decided to walk on the beach, listen to the waves, and look at the stars before going to bed. The walk was really nice and refreshing, the stars and the sea so nice under the moonlight. However, I needed to get to bed to rest for tomorrow.

    I got up early, placing my camera and towel and other things in my bag, and started for the boat. I stopped by the little restaurant to get a quick breakfast, and they gave it to me in a brown bag so I could hurry on to the boat. I arrived at the boat early; however, everything was ready to go. We got a cooler of Singha for the Thais and me from the vendors on the beach. They picked me up in a small boat on the beach to take me out to the larger boat now anchored out in the bay. I climbed aboard and we were ready to leave to catch some fish and have a new adventure. The sun was just rising as I reached the boat; it seemed to rise so slow, then it seemed to suddenly jump into the horizon.

    The small motor on the boat chugged along as we moved closer to the waters where we were going to fish. The boat operator furnished us hand lines to fish with. The day was clear and the waves splashed softly against the boat as we moved along on an enjoyable trip. I finished the ham and egg breakfast that I had gotten earlier. Then we were ready to fish. The Thais cut some bait, and we threw the hand lines over as they let the boat drift with the current. It seemed like a long time just watching the sun rise higher in the sky, but suddenly; we had a fish on one of the hand lines, then on two, and then all four. Smiles came on the Thais faces as we started to pull in the catch: fish from twelve to sixteen inches. We would unhook the fish and throw out the line again, and we continued to catch fish for quite some time. As suddenly as it had started, it stopped. Then it was time for a Singha for all of us. While we were drinking, the Thais asked me what I wanted to do with the fish. I told them they could have them to use, or sell, or whatever they wanted to do with them. It was nearing noon, so the boat captain headed for the island. It was time to rest and to take a few pictures.

When we neared the island, the crew took me ashore to the restaurant for lunch. The islands bay was C-shaped, with a wonderful white sand beach and tropical trees in the background, and the water was as still as a bathtub. The restaurant was just a thatched hut area, where they had no electric. Tables were set up in the sand on thatched mats, with a charcoal cooking area. All the drinks were in coolers, and so was any food that needed to be kept cold. Except for the Singha and sodas, all the remaining food was Thai style. I finally got some charcoal grilled fish with rice and mixed vegetables after pointing and trying to tell the people what I wanted for lunch. They were so pleasant to deal with, it made it really fun. They kept trying to give me extra food long after I was full.

I had my snorkel, facemask, and my camera in its underwater case, and I was ready to go snorkeling. The water was so warm, I wore a t-shirt to keep from getting sunburned. I headed out in search of coral and fish. I reached the area where the coral started as well as quantities of fish. I reached the coral heads, which were only ten to twelve feet deep. However, they were over blessed with fish. In the salt water, one can float on the surface without any effort. The coral was like a living flowerbed; whenever something frightened the fish, they all darted back into the coral, leaving only the coral exposed. As I swam over an area, I saw lots of different things, then when I turned around and swim back over it, I found items I had missed seeing the first time.

I heard a boat coming and I realized I must quickly dive. The long Thai boat that moved over me had the center section cut out and was fitted with a glass window to show the passengers the coral and, in this case, a diver. The boat had a 4-cylinder car engine with a long shaft and an exposed prop at the end. If it had touched me with the prop, I would have been badly cut up. The boat moved off as I swam between the coral heads where the boat could not go, and I started to snorkel again. I was lucky enough to get to see a moray eel and a shark in the distance.

I started taking pictures of the coral and the fish and lost all idea of the time. Then a small boat came my way, and it was the man from the boat I had hired. It was time to go back to the mainland. I crawled into the boat and they took me to our larger boat to head back. We got into the larger boat and the Thais pulled anchor, and we were off to the mainland. I had been out most of the day in the sun with just a t-shirt, and my arms were turning red. I leaned back and was given a Singha and finally realized how tired I was. The clear sky, the splashing water on the boat, and waves rocking the boat was a pleasant way to end the day on the water.

We made it back to the mainland, and the people from the boat got a small boat to take me back to the beach. We all said goodbye on the boat, and I tipped them for the effort they had made for me to have such a good day. I climbed out onto the beach, tired but happy. I was on my way back to the hotel when I remembered to stop at the dive shop. The man said to be at the dive shop at 9:30 in the morning for the refresher course. I continued my walk back to the hotel. I tried to dodge the hawkers whenever I could. However, with me being so dirty, looking like I'd spent the day fishing and swimming, a lot them avoided me anyway.

At the hotel, I took a shower. Washing off the sand and the caked on salt made me feel like a new person. I realized how hungry I was. I thought I would just relax a little on the balcony with a Singha before leaving to get supper. I was able to watch the sun set from my balcony. It was so pleasant watching the swaying trees and the waves with the sun slowly disappearing into them. Soon, only the sound of the waves washing ashore could be heard. The sun had made its descent into the world beyond and would make its reentry in the morning. How wonderful it was to be able to watch the sun rise from the sea in the morning and to watch it set into the sea in the evening. What a wonderful day.

  I changed from my swimming suit and got dressed and headed back to the strip. I walked until I came to a seafood restaurant, located on an old pier. It had two sections; the one in the middle of the pier was air conditioned, and it also housed the kitchen. As you entered the middle section, there were large tanks where one could select a lobster, grouper, or shrimp to eat, if desired. Then I could go to the end section that is open and hear the sound of the waves splashing onto the piling, see the stars, and watch the shrimp boats fill their holds with ice to get ready to go out fishing for shrimp or other seafood.

  I chose the end section and sat down at a table near the end and the edge of the pier. The waitress handed me the menu, and I asked for a Singha, then I looked at the menu. This was one place you could afford to eat lobster! They had a lobster seafood plate, which was what I ordered. Quickly, the waitress returned with my Singha.

  The sky was so clear and the stars shining so brightly that it made for a beautiful evening. I was enjoying the Singha and the ending of a wonderful day. It only seemed like a second until the waitress was back with my lobster. The lobster tasted so good, as it came with a small bowl of fish sauce and lemon juice with hot Thai pepper and garlic cut up in it. I had more than I could eat, even though I had felt so hungry from the day's activities.

  I had just finished my lobster and was finishing eating the other items on the plate when suddenly a shower came up. All the people rushed to get inside. The shower seemed so cooling and nice I just sat there enjoying it and my supper. Having spent so much time in the desert, the shower was really refreshing to me. The waitress came rushing to me with an umbrella holding it over me as I continued to eat. I told her to go inside but she waited there until they brought an umbrella for the table where I was eating. They had no sooner left when the shower was over and my shirt was hardly damp.

I looked out over the sea where I had spent the day fishing, snorkeling, and taking pictures that day. *What a pleasant ending for such a wonderful day*, I thought. With the meal over, I paid my bill and gave the waitress an extra tip for holding the umbrella over me.

I made my way down the strip, walking back to hotel. Although it was after 10:00, I didn't have to get up early in the morning, and I wanted to see how good the Thai bands were in the nightclubs. I made my way past all of the hawkers trying to get me into the nightclubs and walked into the one from which I heard American music coming. The Thai band was good and it was playing American music. I sat at a table toward the back of the club so I could see the dancers in front of the band and the shows they had. Quickly, a waitress came over and took my order for a Singha beer. The headwaiter came back with my Singha beer and set it down in front of me. Then he said, "We have a lot of lovely young ladies that would like to dance with you, would you like me to send over one of the prettiest to dance with you?"

I glanced at my watch and saw it was already after 11:00 and I was tired. "No," I answered. "I am tired and have to start my diving class tomorrow." Shortly after the waiter left, a girl who had been dancing came over to my table and asked if she could sit down. I nodded my head and she sat down. Then she asked for a drink, and I had the waitress bring her one. They knew what drink she wanted without asking.

When we began talking, the band started to play a really good song, and the lady asked if that I want to dance. Again, I nod my head and we move to the dance floor and began dancing. When the first song ended, we continued dancing with the next song they were playing. Then they started to play a slow song and we continued dancing. The perfumed smell of the soft-skinned Thai girl I held close to me dancing, with her wonderful smile, was a exciting way to end an evening. The combination of the Singhas and the long day caught up to me. It was an perfect ending to the evening in Pattaya.

I glanced at my watch again and it was after midnight. We went back to our table, and I tried to excuse myself from the girl. She hung on and said that she wanted to go with me. I finally told her I was too tired and left for the hotel. As I walked back on the strip, the clubs were still going full blast; not like Bangkok, where they closed up at midnight. Finally, I got past the clubs and all the noise. Walking along the beach, I can hear the waves gently splashing ashore, picturing how the sand moved, with all the crabs running to return to the sea as each new wave came in. With the stars and the moon overhead to show me the way and a light breeze in my face to keep me cool, I thought, *What more could you ask for?*

I finally reached my hotel, and, crawling into bed, I thought briefly about the workers I had left behind in Saudi Arabia, with the hot weather and the blowing sand and the high humidity. After that, I quickly slid off to sleep.

I woke up late, feeling good after spending yesterday on the sea. I shaved, cleaned up, and – for some reason – I was really hungry. After getting dressed, I went to the German restaurant where I had eaten before. I wanted to try the ham and eggs they had. So as soon as I found a place to sit, the waitress came over to take my order. I ordered the ham and eggs with some orange juice and hot tea. They brought back the orange juice, and in a short time, I got the remaining part of my order. It was really good to get some nice food cooked properly. Breakfast finished, I headed to the dive shop.

At the dive shop, the instructor wanted to know if I had ever dived before. "Yes," I told him, "I was certified in California in 1968 by both NAUII and Los Angles County. I do not have my certification or my dive log with me."

The other people were gathered as we moved to the pool for the diving check out. The instructor explained about the diving equipment and how to use the correct weight to allow you to slowly descend. The instructor showed us how to clear our facemask and our regulator. Then we went to the pool to test how much we had learned. We put on our weight belts, facemasks, flippers, tanks, and regulators and were allowed to swim around the pool under water. Our facemasks, tanks, and regulators were placed at the deep end of the pool, and each person had to dive to get them on and clear their equipment.

Everybody was successful except for one lady. Some of the guys had brought along their Thai girl friends. Before we were all finished, it was close to 1:30. The instructor informed us to meet at the dive shop at 8:00 tomorrow morning to go on the dive. Then we went our separate ways.

I had been talked with one of the guys taking the refresher course; he had a boat being built close by and was going to it after lunch. We walked down the strip a short way to the restaurant he said was good. He said the hamburgers were really good there, so I decided to try one with a Singha and so did he. The waitress came, we gave her our orders, and she rushed off to get them.

I talked to the man from the dive class. He was a seaman and had sailed around the world on all kinds of freighters. He got sick on one and was put off at Singapore to go to the hospital. He quickly recovered and found that Singapore outfits all kinds of boats in the outer docks cheaper than anyplace else. He had come here to get a boat built and planned to take it to Singapore and get it fully outfitted. Then he would sell it in Singapore or sail it to California and sell it. He said he made twice as much doing that as he did as a seaman on the freighters.

Soon our hamburgers arrived and we started eating. He asked about me, and I told him how I worked overseas and I was there on R & R from Saudi Arabia. He told me some bad experiences he'd had while unloading in the Arab ports, and he didn't miss going back to them. By that time, we were finished eating; I paid for the meal and we headed back to the strip.

We found a taxi to take us to the area where they were building his sailboat. We went down the road to see it, driving around the twisting road around the bay to a sheltered area where they built boats. We came to an almost completed boat, and the taxi stopped and let us off. We walked up to the boat, which was a wooden sailboat about forty feet long. As we went aboard, I noticed that it had a lot of teak in the deck and the cabins had lots of hand carved teak in them. He said the sails were not good and would only be used on the trip to Singapore.

In Singapore, they would put on better sails as well as an automatic steering system and lot of other items to be able to make it more saleable, with the proper winches for the sails and all the other items needed that he cannot get here in Thailand. He will not know until he gets it outfitted in Singapore if he will sell it there or sail it to California. It would really be a wonderful boat when he got it finished. Then he took me down to the harbor to look at another boat that was being built there.

This was something different; I had seen them before in California, but not since. It had a special design of concrete used to make the hull; rebar was formed over the boat hull, which was covered with a release agent as well as plastic to ensure it was released. Then the concrete was shot on the hull (like they do on a swimming pool). The concrete was then spray cured with water or steam to ensure it dried properly. This boat was about thirty-two feet long. It was nice to see the boats. I wanted one, but I did not have the experience needed to sail one. The seaman said he would teach me.

We said our goodbyes and that we would see each other on the dive trip tomorrow. I went to the road to catch a taxi; soon a taxi came along and let out somebody coming from Pattaya and that was my chance to get back to Pattaya. It was dark before I reached Pattaya.

The little taxi reached Pattaya and stopped at my hotel. It was time to shower and get ready to go out to supper. A warm shower really felt good. Soon I was dressed and ready to go out for supper.

I walked down the strip and came to a steak house run by an American. "I think I will have a steak tonight," I said to myself, as I walked into the restaurant. Soon a waitress came to seat me. She provided me with a menu and asked what that I wanted to drink. "Give me a Singha" I responded to her. She told me she would get my drink while I made my selection from the menu. I selected the T-bone steak, baked potato, salad, and mixed vegetables.

When she returned with my drink, I gave her my order, then she asked, "How do you want it cooked?"

"Well done," was my reply, and she went to place my order.

The restaurant was outside under a covered roof. The cool sea breeze kept it cool with help from the ceiling fan and other well placed fans around the restaurant. I was enjoying my Singha and the evening when my steak arrived. This was really the first Western meal I'd had since being in Thailand except for the hamburgers. The steak was really good and not a tough old water buffalo like some had told me they'd gotten when ordering a steak here. I finished my steak and was just finishing my Singha when the waitress came to ask about dessert. I was so full, I did not want any more, so I paid her. I walked out of the restaurant and onto the strip.

I started toward my hotel when I passed the club I'd been in last night. I decided to go in for a nightcap. I found the same table I'd had the night before and sat down to listen to the music. The waitress came over and asked what I wanted to drink. I said, "Please give me a Singha." And she walked off to get my order. They had a different band playing that night. I had expected to see the girl I danced with the night before; however, I could not find her.

The waitress brought my drink, and I realized how tired I was. It was nice to sit and watch the people dance, though. There were several Thai girls who were dancing with each other, hoping for somebody to cut in on their dance. I thought about cutting in on the girls, but decided to just finish my beer and go back to the hotel tonight. I finished my drink and walked back along the strip to the hotel. Passing the beach was always a pleasant time when the weather was so nice. Soon I was at the hotel, into my room, turned out the lights and was quickly asleep.

In the morning, I got up and got ready to go. I left the hotel with my bag of dive equipment and went to where the German had his restaurant. That morning it was bacon, eggs, and toast, with orange juice and tea. I gave my order to the waitress when she came. Then she went off to get it. Soon, I was eating breakfast. I was going to miss all this good food when I left there the next day. With breakfast finished, it was time to go down the strip to the dive shop. I got to the dive shop early and helped the instructor load the diving gear onto the boat.

The boat was a regular Thai fishing boat; however, they had added an access ladder to get into the boat. Soon, the other people arrived from the class the day before. When everybody was accounted for, we left. This would be my first dive in a very long time. I enjoyed the boat ride out to the dive spot and talked the seaman about his boat and how he was going to have it fixed up to sell. All too quickly, we reached the dive spot. Before anybody got ready, we went over the procedures again with the instructor. Then everybody got on their masks, snorkels, fins, weight belts, tanks, and regulators. Then we were told about the Thai glass bottom boats; when we saw them, we were to dive to the bottom so their props could not hit us.

Then we all went over the side into the water and headed for the bottom. As soon as we reached the bottom, the instructor came along, making sure we had all cleared our ears, and we gave him the "OK" sign by holding out thumb and forefinger together in a circle. We were to follow him as we swam about thirty feet under water. He pointed out different items in the coral and fish to us. All too quickly, we reached the end of our air supply. I slowly returned to the surface, allowing for decompression by returning to the surface slower than our air bubbles from our breathing.

We surfaced a short distance from the boat and swam to the boat to board. We rested for a while on the boat, then we paired off and made a dive with our partners. The seaman was my partner, and we got suited up and jumped overboard for the last dive of the day. The water was so clear and warm, it made for wonderful diving. We swam along the bottom, finding seashells and other items that were really nice to look at. The colorful fish were always nice to watch.

Our air supply was depleted a lot more quickly than our desire to explore. Soon it was time to return to the boat, where we enjoyed the lunch that was packed by our instructor. Everybody was hungry and there was no bickering about not wanting this or that at lunch. Questions were asked and answered about our dive. Then the instructor passed out the certification for the dive and t-shirts, and we left for the mainland and the dive shop.

It was another really nice day to be out on the sea, but my arms had just had too much sun, as had my back; although I had on a t-shirt, the sun and salt managed to get through and I had a really good sunburn. Soon our boat was anchoring back in the bare beach spot.

I decided to stay a while in the shade on one of the lounges the hawkers rented on the beach. It felt so good to just lay down and relax for a while. Soon hawkers on the beach provided me a Singha and I was ready to relax and enjoy. I stayed on the beach to watch the sun go down and until the mosquitoes arrived. Then it was time to walk back up the strip to my hotel.

As I walked back up the strip, the clubs were starting to come alive again. The lights were on and the music was coming out of the clubs. I finally got to the section of beach were the strip ended just before the hotel. When I made it to the hotel, the shower never looked or felt so good. It was really nice to get the caked salt off and have some cool water on the sunburn. With the shower finished, I got dressed and then had to make the decision where I would eat that night. Why not seafood on my last night at Pattaya?

I left the hotel to go to the same seafood restaurant where I had eaten before. I walked down the strip to the seafood restaurant and entered it. I passed the large glass tanks where you could pick your own seafood and passed through the air-conditioned area out to the open area. I found a table in the corner, where I could view the sea and the fishing boats leaving as well as look at the stars.

I sat down to wait on the waitress. It was not long before she arrived with the menu for me, then she took my drink order, which was a Singha, and went back to get it as I checked the menu. There was a seafood combination plate with lobster, shrimp, crab, grouper, as well as other items. I decided on that for my last supper in Pattaya this trip. When the waitress returned with my Singha, I gave her my order and waited for it to arrive. I was tired from the dive trip that day.

The stars looked so bright, I could pick out some of the constellations. I watched the boats loading ice to go out for their catch. I wondered if some time I could catch a ride on one of those boats just to watch them use their nets at night. Then my seafood plate arrived.

I had a lot to eat. It all tasted so good, and the Thai sauce added a special taste to the seafood. The lobster, crab, and other items tasted so special tonight. I knew that I would really miss that food. All too soon, I was full and my plate was not near empty. Again, my eyes were bigger than my belly.

I finished my Singha and paid and tipped the waitress and started out of the restaurant and onto the strip. I walked down the strip and came to the club again where I had met the girl the first night. I walked in and found the table I had the first visit; it was empty and the waitress led me to it. As I sat down, the waitress asked what I wanted to drink, and I told her a Singha, so she went to the bar to get it. As she did, I got a chance to look around the club.

The same band was playing that had been playing the first night. They were a really good band. The waitress got back with my Singha and I paid and tipped her and she left with hardly any conversation; usually, they would try to push their girls on a customer. I could not find the girl I met the first night there and decided to finish my beer and turn in for the evening after getting packed for tomorrow.

Then it happened: a girl who was about as pretty as the south end of a northbound horse came to my table. What she lacked in beauty, she made up for in personality. She asked if she could sit down, which was a change. I had to say "yes". As she sat down, I told her that I was tired and was about to leave. It did not bother her at all. I guessed that she was used to being brushed off. She asked if I would buy her a drink and I said yes, waving the waitress over to our table. She already knew what to bring to the table so she first stopped by the bar and picked up the drink for the girl.

As the waitress the arrived with the drink, the girl told me that her name was Yeu. I told her my name and we went through the usual "where are you from" and "what do you do" questions. Then she asked me to dance. I told her I was tired but would dance one dance with her, and then I had to go back to the hotel. She was a really good dancer and I enjoyed dancing with her. We talked about Thailand and all of the things that were going on while we danced, then we danced another dance. We sat down and finished another round of drinks. Then she asked if I wanted to take her back to my hotel room. I told her I was just too tired, but I liked her and gave her some money. Then told her I was leaving tomorrow for Bangkok.

"That is all right," she said. "I can go with you. I can show you plenty of sites in Bangkok."

I said, "No, thanks, because I was meeting somebody in Bangkok." Finally, that seemed to satisfy her and she got up when I did to walk with me to the door. When we went outside onto the strip she grabbed me and gave me a really big kiss. I was really surprised! Then she turned and walked back into the club.

I walked down the strip by the beach area back to my hotel. The night was so wonderful, the stars so bright and the sound of the waves on the beach so tranquil. Back in my hotel room, I packed to get ready for my trip to back to Bangkok the next day.

Chapter 8: Back to Bangkok

I woke to a bright sunny day, and got dressed and packed the last things I had spared out to use that morning. I went to breakfast before checking out of the hotel and catching the bus to Bangkok. I went downstairs and walked down the strip to the German's place since they had good food. I sat down and the waitress came to my table and handed me the menu. I selected the ham and eggs with toast, orange juice, and hot tea. I was sad to leave Pattaya, but all vacations must come to an end. I ate my breakfast and went back to the hotel to check out.

Back at the hotel, I went upstairs to my room to get my bags and took the elevator downstairs to check out. When I reached the reception desk, I gave them my key, and since I had already told them I would be checking out, they had gotten me a bus back to Bangkok today. I paid my bill and then sat down in the lobby to wait for the bus to Bangkok.

The bus arrived at the hotel and I had one more look around to see all of the things I would remember about Pattaya. The strip, the beach, the sea, the boat...the list could go on for a very long time. I took my suitcase and walked to the bus. The bus driver had the luggage door open and I gave him my ticket and my suitcase to place under the bus in the luggage compartment. Then I boarded the bus. This was the last pickup point for the bus and we were soon going down the strip to get back to the highway to Bangkok. Traffic was light on the strip this early in the morning and we made good time going down the strip. The strip ends and the section of beach appeared where some of the Thai fishing boats were still anchored. I guessed they were not booked or had an afternoon booking.

The bus moved out onto the main highway. I would have hated to drive in Thailand; the drivers were polite and all, but drove on the wrong side of the road and there was just so much traffic in Bangkok. The Thai buses were different than the ones I had ridden in the States. They had a hostess (like an airplane stewardess) who came around and took orders for drinks as well as served a snack on the way to Bangkok. Soon, she was at my seat and I ordered a Singha to enjoy the bus ride with. The hostess was soon back with it, and I paid and tipped her and continued to watch the scenery out the window.

We passed the Chinese graves and the Buddhist Temple on the hill as we continued into Bangkok. We reached the wind-powered pumps that pump water to irrigate the fields; this always amazed me. I could remember these landmarks as we continued our trip back to Bangkok. It was not long before we were into heavy traffic as we reached the divided four lane section of traffic near Bangkok, surrounded by the stands selling the really large crabs with their claws tied with bamboo strips.

We crossed the main river that the rice barges follow down to the gulf, bringing back whatever that they can to Bangkok. Building materials were one of the many items that they brought back up the river.

We arrived in Bangkok as I finished my second Singha. I got it when the hostess served the snacks at the midpoint of our trip. As we neared the bus terminal in Bangkok, the traffic was really terrible. The hotel I stayed in before was fully booked, so they had booked me in a different hotel that they own to stay the remaining three days of my vacation. Soon the bus stopped at the terminal and we unloaded. I got my luggage and found a taxi to take me to my hotel. The taxi driver loaded my luggage, and we agreed on a price when I told him what hotel I would be going to. We were off to the hotel, and it did not seem too far. I checked into the hotel and was taken to my room.

I stored my luggage and then it was time for lunch. I got my slip for the shirts being made for me at the tailor shop and planned to get lunch at the same time. I went downstairs to the lobby, stopping by the reception desk. I asked the lady at the desk to check for Emma's name in the Thai phone book, hoping somebody different could find it. I offered her 40 baht to check and she said she would. I then left the lobby.

Outside of the hotel, I found a taxi and bargained on the price to go to the tailor shop. When the price was agreed upon, I got into the taxi to go to the tailor shop. Moving through the Bangkok streets, it was now very slow, as the streets were congested. We arrived at the tailor shop and I went in to get my shirts. That was where I began a new adventure.

When I stepped into the tailor shop, it started. I entered the tailor shop and the Thai gentleman remembered me. "I have your shirts ready," he said as he saw me enter the shop. He disappeared into the back of the shop and came back with a package, handing it to me.

"I need to try on the shirts you have made for me," I said.

"Yes, yes," he said, nodding and speaking at the same time as he unwrapped the package. He ushered me to a section of the small store that was screened off for fittings. I took off my shirt as he handed me one he had made. I tried on the shirt and discovered that the shirts had been tapered instead of being made full – the shirt would not button over my belly. The tailor looked very surprised at the shirt not fitting. I told the tailor I was leaving and wanted my money back or a shirt that fits. The tailor called the shop that made the shirts. Many of these tailor shops were only store fronts; I learned that they have the sewing contracted out to small shops around town. There was a rapid exchange of Thai over the telephone for a long time. The tailor turned to me and asked that I pay him the remaining part of the money for the shirts. He would have his driver take me to the shop that would fix the shirts while I waited, then I would not have to come back to his shop. I told him if they didn't fix the shirts, I would be back.

"No worry, no worry, they fix very good," he said, as he wrote a note in Thai to take with me to the shop to fix my shirts. He gave me the note and the package of shirts and I paid him the remaining money. Then I followed the driver out the back to his car.

When we got out back, there was no car – only a blue motor scooter. I must have looked as surprised as a kid caught with his hand in a cookie jar. I looked at him, and he looked at me, and finally I started to laugh. He spoke no English; I spoke no Thai. There was a small stand that sold noodles and drinks near his scooter. I motioned to him to come sit down, as I ordered by pointing for two Singhas before we took off to get the shirts fixed. The Thai lady brought over the Singhas and I also got a small bottle of Mekong, a brand of Thai whiskey that just fits in my shirt pocket. When we finished the Singhas, we went over to his scooter and he got on and started it. Then I climbed aboard behind him, took a sip of the Mekong, and we were off to get my shirts fixed.

We buzzed down the back alleys and streets, missing people, dogs, cats, and vendors pushing carts, and weaving in and out of cars. We got a lot of stares from everyone as we zoomed down the streets on the scooter. A Thai on a scooter was no new sight to the Thais, but an American twice his size hanging on behind him with a package and sipping Mekong from a bottle made a new sight for them. The only thing I really remembered passing was the Indra Hotel, and shortly after that, we stopped. I followed the scooter operator through all kinds of sewing machines, material, cutting boards, and busy workers sewing all kind of different items.

Finally, we arrived at an older Thai lady's shop, and I pulled out from my shirt pocket the note the tailor had given to me along with the Mekong bottle for a drink. I passed the note to the lady along with the package. As she looked at the note, I knew that she was unable to read it, although it was in Thai. She looked at the note and was very puzzled as to what it said. The scooter operator only knew he was to take me here but did not know why. I tried to explain in my best sign language what need to be done. The sign language was not making matters better; it only seemed to make matters worse.

The Thai ladies working on the sewing machines were busy pointing and laughing at us. The Thai lady and the little scooter operator were talking so fast and loud I though they were going to come to blows. Neither understood English or seemed to understand what I was trying to tell them, and neither could read Thai to understand the note from the tailor.

Finally, one of the young Thai ladies from behind one of the sewing machines walked up to us and asked, "May I help you?"

I was very surprised to hear some English spoken. I looked at her and said, "I am leaving shortly and the shirts that you made for me do not fit." Then I continued, "They sent me with this note telling what is wrong with the shirts." I handed the note to the girl, saying, "They sent me here to get the shirts corrected so that I can take them with me." She read the note, then I showed her how the shirts had been tapered instead of being full. She eyed me very carefully because my arms were peeling from the sunburn I had gotten swimming and diving at Pattaya.

The young Thai lady turned to the older Thai lady and spoke. There was a rapid exchange of the Thai language in the triangle of speech between the three of them. The young Thai lady turned to me and said in a very pleasant voice, "It will take about a one half hour to fix the shirts; can you come back in one half hour?"

"Come back in a half hour – I don't even know where I am!" I said. Then I added, "Besides, it is lunch time; we can go to lunch then come back." I was not about to let the scooter driver leave me here on my own until I got my shirts and knew where I was. I told the young Thai lady to tell the scooter driver to take me to lunch then bring me back here to get my shirts.

"No, no," he said, and I could understand that. Then he went on in Thai, saying he had to leave. However, it was finally agreed for him to take me to lunch, then bring me back. He talked to the Thais at the sewing shop and off we went to eat at a Thai restaurant that was close by. I got some fried noodles and he got some kind of shrimp soup with rice. By the time we finished our meals and had a beer, it was time to go back for the shirts.

When we came back, the older Thai lady had gone to lunch. However, the younger Thai lady who spoke English was there. I asked her to let me try on the shirts, and they all fit the way they were supposed to.

"What is your name?" I asked the young Thai lady.

"My name is Dow, and what is your name?" she asked.

"They all call me Ed," I responded, as they wrapped up the shirts for me.

Then I tried my best charm on the young Thai lady. "How about going out to supper with me?" I asked her.

She was very polite, shook her head no, smiled, and kept busy.

Then I tried again. "I am leaving soon; we could go out together tonight for supper, dancing, or go to the movies, whatever you want to do." The Thai scooter driver

75

was smiling, almost laughing, as he seemed to know what I was asking and that I was being turned down. Then I took a 100 baht note and gave it to the young Thai lady and said, "I will wait until 7:00PM at my hotel for you." I handed her a card from the hotel so she would know where to meet me. I wrote my room number on the card. "Use the money to get a taxi to the hotel." I did get a maybe, but not a firm yes from her. "At 7:00PM at my hotel." I said to her again as I waved goodbye.

I had the scooter operator leave me at the Indra Hotel so I could shop and look around. Then he was going to go back to the tailor shop. Anyway, I had my shirts and a maybe date tonight.

I wandered around the shopping center with all the different kinds of shops. One could get eyeglasses made, suits made, jewelry made. It even had a post office in the basement. I bought some cards and sent them out from the post office. At the back of the center was a Patta Store. I wandered around in it and found a leather case just the right size to hold my passport and my shot record card and bought it. I still have that passport holder.

I was out of film, so I got some more film. Upstairs they had a movie theater. There was a Chinese movie playing in the theater that was in English and made in Hong Kong. They had some really marvelous leap scenes in the movie. It was a really fast moving movie with lots of fighting scenes also. Going to a movie in Thailand was a real experience. One selects the seat desired when buying the ticket and is then escorted to the seat by an usher. At the start of the movie, they play the Thai national anthem and everybody stands as they show pictures of the flag, the king, the queen, and the king's mother. When the show was finished, I walked outside to find a taxi to get back to my hotel. It was rush hour and the traffic was moving really slowly – so slowly you could count the ants on the sidewalk.

We arrived at the hotel and I stopped by the lobby to see if the Thai lady had found Emma in the phone book. She told me she'd had no luck. I asked her if there was any way she knew I could find Emma. She suggested the police, but I did not think that was a wise choice, so I thanked her and went to my room. After showering and dressing, I went down to the lobby to meet the Thai lady. By the time I got to the lobby, it was already 7:15. Had I missed her? Did she just take the 100 baht and forget to come? I wondered what was happening. All dressed, I thought maybe I should check with the reception desk to see if she came there. I went to the reception desk and asked if she had stopped by. There was a young Thai girl at the reception desk. I asked if anybody had inquired if I was in. Very politely, she said, "You had no callers".

Now it was after 7:30. However, it was raining like Noah's flood outside. I turned to look at the clock above the reception desk hoping my watch was wrong, but it also had 7:30 on it. *Well, I guess she is not coming*, I thought. I stood and checked the clock one more time, hoping she would walk through the door. Just then, as suddenly as it started, it stopped raining. As I turned to leave, like a star in the night, this beautiful young Thai lady entered the hotel front door. It was like having a ship come in that had been missing for a long time. As I approached her, she smelled like a lily in a field of new blooms, and looked like an orchid in a snowstorm. This was my date for tonight. Like a lion rushing to get a newborn impala, I rushed to the Thai lady from the sewing shop, meeting her just as she came through the hotel entrance.

"Hi, Dow," I said to her. "I was really afraid you would not come. Would you want to eat here since it is raining?" I asked politely.

"I don't really care," she replied. "If you like Mexican food, I know a restaurant that you may like."

"I like Mexican food," I replied, wondering what this restaurant would be like.

We walked out of the hotel and Dow took my hand. "Follow me," she said, as we walked past the hotel taxis to the familiar old blue Datsun. She talked to the first taxi driver, then walked back to the second taxi and talked to that driver. After a few seconds of bargaining, she turned to me and said, "We can go with him for 50 baht." So I paid the taxi driver, and we both slid into the back seat of the taxi. The taxi then pulled out into the rush of traffic. I turned to Dow and asked why she had passed up the first taxi.

"He wanted 100 baht because you are a foreigner," she replied.

As the taxi crawled along through the traffic, we exchanged small talk, asking all the usual questions. We found out both of our birthdays are on the tenth of the month, which I thought was strange. We seemed to have a lot in common.

We arrived at the same Mexican restaurant I had been to before. Our taxi door was opened by a fully uniformed doorman, the same one who was only 3 feet tall. We received a really big greeting when he said "Welcome," to us in his best English. He escorted us to the restaurant door, opened it for us, and bowed as we entered the restaurant. (I learned that the Thai like to try new restaurants and many flock to the new ones that open, then when the newness wears off, they are abandoned and many close, only to start again as a new restaurant.)

We walked into the restaurant and were escorted to a table. A nice looking Thai waitress soon came to our table. She asked what we wanted to drink as she passed us the menus to select from.

I ordered a Singha beer as usual and Dow selected orange juice. The waitress left to get our drinks as we looked through the menu, which was in both Thai and English. They had a special, which had a mixture of Mexican food on it. When the waitress returned with our drinks, we gave her our order of two of the specials, and she left to place the order. We were seated next to a window and could see that the heavens were still open and the rain still coming down like the forty days noted in the bible with Noah.

I asked Dow what her complete name was. Then she explained to me a lot of Thais go by nicknames and she said that Dow was a nickname that meant "star" in Thai. She told me her real name was Poungkeaw. Then I asked her what her last name was and she told me it was Promma. I asked her if I could see her name written out in English. She took a card from her purse and it had her name in Thai and in English, Poungkeaw Promma. I showed her my name on a company ID card I had with my picture on it.

We continued to talk, and it seemed like only seconds before our order was brought to our table. You have to remember where you are when you select food that is not from the original place. As for Mexican food in Bangkok, I thought it was very good. The company I was with made the food even taste better. By the time we had finished eating, it was after 9:00 PM. I asked Dow if she wanted to go dancing and learned that she loved to dance. We walked out of the restaurant and were again greeted by the midget doorman, whom I tipped as he stopped a taxi for us.

The rain stopped as suddenly as it had started when we reached the taxi. We both climbed in the back of the taxi and Dow bartered with the taxi driver to get the best price. The little blue Datsun looked really good shining in the fresh rain and under the lights of the restaurant. The price was agreed to and we were off to go dancing. The air was so clean and fresh after being washed with the rain. The Thai taxi drivers were so polite, allowing other cars to cut in front of them and never giving them a cussing like Americans would.

As we drove to the dance hall, we saw a car had overturned on the slick streets from the heavy rain. A police car was there when we passed the accident. It seemed like only a short time after the accident that we reached the place where we were to go dancing. Thai Heaven looked busy and I asked Dow if she was sure that she wanted to go here, remembering Lee. However, I stood no chance of getting her to change her mind. The taxi stopped, and we started for the entrance as the doorman opened the door for us.

Once we were in Thai Heaven, a waitress ushered us to a table and we ordered drinks. I ordered a Singha and Dow ordered a mixed drink. It was mostly dark with the light from the stage where the Thai band was playing. The band was a good band, and it was nice to be in a place where you could sit back and relax. The next song the band played was one that I knew.

I got up and asked Dow to dance. We were soon out on the floor dancing. The dance floor was very crowded, and we keep bumping into people, but nobody seemed to mind and we were having fun dancing. The band changed to a slow song, during which we could dance and talk together. Dow's freshly washed hair smelled so good, and she had on the best smelling perfume. We were talking and continued dancing even after the band had stopped playing.

The band had stopped playing as it was time for the Thai boxing event to take place. Out came the mats and the ring was set up on the dance floor. Then out came the Thai boxers. Each time they boxed, they had a routine they went through, praying and honoring their teachers. As is the custom, we each selected our favorite fighter. Dow liked red, so she selected the fighter in the red trunks. I got the fighter in the blue trunks. Later, I was to learn that Dow's favorite color is red and that is why that she chose that fighter. We bet 100 baht on the fight.

I always enjoyed Thai kickboxing. It was so different from stateside boxing. The match soon started along with the Thai music that went with the fighting. The fighters came from their corners, and the fighter in the red shorts soon placed a kick to the blue boxer's side that sent him to the mat. After three quick rounds, the fight was over, but no winner was declared. However, both Dow and I agreed that the fighter in the red trunks had fought the best fight, so I paid her the 100 baht.

They took down the ring and rolled up the mat. Back came the band to continue the music. The bump was still popular at that time, and we danced to the music and did the bump. Then another slow song was played. It was really nice to hold somebody who was soft and warm and smelled like a lady should smell. Her long black hair fluttered like a flower in the wind as she danced.

Then the lights came on again and it was time for the traditional Thai dancers to come on the dance floor. The musicians who played the music for the Thai dance came out, dressed in ancient Thai dress, and they started playing. At the start of the music, the Thai dancers came out. They wore the long brass on their fingers to represent the long fingernails of the old Thai dancers. However, tonight they had several very young dancers who were learning the classic Thai dance to keep the Thai traditions alive. It was nice to see the young girls trying so hard to perform like their ancestors did. Soon the dance was over and the dancers left the floor.

Back came the band and we were back on the dance floor dancing to a song that I knew. We returned to the table to get a drink and take a short rest before we returned to the dance floor. Then a photographer came to our table to take a picture. We agreed to let him take our picture and the photographer took the photo. It was a Polaroid camera and we soon received the picture from the photographer. As we were looking at the picture, the lights came on, all too early, ending our evening at Thai Heaven. Everybody seemed to leave but only halfheartedly.

Out on the street, the rain that had stopped was now back. It seemed to persist this time. It left large puddles in the road and sidewalk. We weaved in and out to miss the puddles as Dow led me to a nearby noodle stand. They seemed to have these stands outside of all the movies and clubs and do a really good business when the people come out of those establishments.

The Thais seemed to eat six times a day: first, breakfast, and then a snack between breakfast and lunch, then lunch, and then a snack between lunch and supper, then supper, then the last snack after supper and before bed time, but they don't seem to get fat eating all these meals. I guessed it was the amount that was eaten compared to the work that was done that makes someone fat. They usually only eat a small quantity at each meal, though. This also seemed to protect them from getting ulcers, unlike their Western counterparts. Also, maybe it is their pleasant attitude that helps them keep the ulcers away.

Dow spoke to the hawker and got us two bowls of noodles with mushrooms. We found a place to sit down out of the rain so we could eat.

After finishing our noodles, we walked back to the road to catch a taxi. Because of the rain, we had a hard time getting a taxi. Finally, we were able to flag down one of the little blue Datsun taxis. Dow made the usual agreement about payment before we got into the taxi, and we went back to the hotel. We talked about all the fun that we'd had that night. Not wanting it to end, I wanted to know when I could see her again. She talked about meeting me the following night. I wanted to meet her for lunch; finally, she agreed to meet me for lunch at the Indra Hotel and then go to a movie. Then we would see afterward what we would do.

The taxi arrived at my hotel and I kissed Dow goodnight. I gave her money for the taxi and to meet me for lunch tomorrow. I climbed out of the taxi and stood to watch it drive out of sight, into the traffic and the rain. Dow waved out the back window to me. Finally, the light was gone and I realized just how lonely I was. Divorced twelve years before, college, work, and distance had kept me from getting involved again until now.

I walked into the hotel and decided to check again to see if the receptionist that was on duty had found any clues to help me locate Emma. Of all the calls she had made, nobody knew Emma. I went to the elevator and took it up to my room. I entered into my room, undressed, and got into bed thinking about lunch tomorrow.

Chapter 9: Another Beginning

The bright sun shining in the window woke me. It was morning and I did not realize that I had slept so late. I got up, went to the bathroom and shaved, washed, and then got dressed. I went downstairs to eat breakfast. I had selected a nice table by the window so I could watch all the people going by. The waitress came over with a menu for me. *Gee! Another selection to make*, I thought.

"I will try the pancakes this morning with some bacon, orange juice and hot tea," I told the waitress, who soon hurried off to get my order. The waitress came back with my order, as I watched the people on the street hurrying home or to work or wherever. There were all sizes and shapes in all kinds of dress; people from China, India, Burma, Viet Nam, England, and every now and then, an American. During the Viet Nam war, the Americans had many airbases in Thailand. They used these bases to bomb the sites in Viet Nam.

When the war ended in Viet Nam, the Thailand students were afraid that the United States would pull out of Thailand like they did in Viet Nam, and Thailand would be taken over by the communists. The United States had done this in Viet Nam, Cambodia, and Laos. The students threw rocks at the military's tanks and were finally able to persuade the Thai government to have all of the United States military leave their bases in Thailand.

I finished breakfast, paid for it, and walked out to the lobby and then to the street to get a taxi. I was going to the bookstore in the Indra Shopping Center.

By that time, I was getting used to the traffic, or maybe just more accustomed to it anyway. We drove through the heavily trafficked streets as we made our way to the Indra Shopping Center. It had a hotel, movie theaters, and all kinds of shops and restaurants. We arrived in front of the Indra Center, and I was able to get out amid the unloading and loading of buses and other taxis. I hurried up the stairs to get inside the shopping center. I walked through the corridors, passing all the little hawkers selling all kinds of souvenirs and trinkets, until I finally arrived at the bookstore.

The store had a good selection of books. I selected one on Thai history, which was written by a local Thai professor. I usually tried to find a book that was written by local historians, because they seemed to be better written and more informative. I selected a Thai cookbook and a couple more books. Then I noticed that it was already after 11:30.

I hurried to the restaurant area in the Indra hotel to meet Dow. I settled down to wait. I knew it was early. Then I wondered, *What if she does not show up?* I had done this before and was stood up, and it did not matter or bother me; however, this time with Dow, it seemed to bother me for some strange reason. I kept glancing at my watch to see if the time had come, but it seemed that time was standing still as I waited. I kept looking at the door and then checking my watch. Each time a Thai lady would enter, I would strain my eyes to see if it was Dow. As the double doors opened again, Dow appeared. I rushed down to meet her. I thought we would eat in the restaurant in the Indra;

85

however, Dow said she knew of a new restaurant that she wanted to try. I said that was fine with me.

"However," she added, "we could eat here if you do not want to go to the new restaurant."

"No, that will be fine," I said, and we walked outside to get a taxi. After the usual barter for the price, we were soon in a taxi headed to the new restaurant. The traffic was really heavy at this time of day in Bangkok. As the taxi slowly wound its way through the maze of traffic, we talked about last night. We talked about the restaurant, the food, the dancing, and the weather. Finally, the taxi pulled over to a newly opened Thai restaurant. We got out of the taxi and proceeded toward the restaurant.

The restaurant was newly opened and the signs still shone with newly painted pictures and letters. The waitress met us at the door and then ushered us to a table near the window. We were seated and provided with menus. We looked at the menus and we each selected something different. I selected a salad with the steak; Dow, a noodle dish and a rice dish. The waitress asked what kind of salad dressing I would like, and I told her French, and she returned with our drinks and my salad with Thousand Island dressing. I asked the waitress if she could bring French or Italian dressing, and, taking the bottle, she left. Later, another man came back with the same bottle of Thousand Island dressing. When I realized they only *had* Thousand Island dressing, I took the bottle and smiled at the waiter.

The Oriental people are different; if you order something they do not have, they do not want to tell you they do not have it, but bring you something else hoping you will be satisfied with what they have brought to you, instead of what you had ordered.

Our food was brought to our table, and as we talked, we ate. The food was really good, I was surprised to note. We watched the happenings on the Bangkok street as we ate. We finished eating and continued talking long after the food was gone. The waitress had brought us our check, and she came back to remind us that we have finished eating and we needed to leave, though she was very polite about it.

    Dow said it was only a short walk to the movies from the restaurant as I tried to get a taxi, so we could walk and would not need a taxi. We were early, so we stopped at a couple of shops along the way. They had jewelry and things for women, so I was able to buy something for my mother and my sister.

    Finally, we arrived at the movie. We went to the ticket window where Dow selected where she wanted to sit. The prices of the seats varied according to where one sits. I purchased the tickets, and since we had just finished eating, we did not get any popcorn or drinks. We went to a James Bond 007 movie. We both liked these movies and would see many more in the future.

    We went to the inside of the theater and were taken to our seats by the usher. We sat down and watched the previews. When the movie was about to start, the national anthem was played while everybody stood while pictures of the King and Queen and the King's mother were shown. The movie started and we enjoyed a nice film. I was glad Dow understood English so well.

    When the movie was over, the lights came on, and everybody headed to the exits to leave the theater. The people poured out onto the sidewalk. We had reservations tonight for a Thai restaurant, which had a show of classical dancing and original Thai food. It was only 5:30PM, and the reservations are not until 7:00PM, but I wanted to get some fast speed film to shoot in the low light conditions. So we got a taxi and went back to the Indra Shopping center. We went to the camera department and got some 1000 ASA film for my camera. Then I was ready for the show. Dow found a couple of items she needed and I paid for them and we were on our way.

We went outside and found a taxi just as it was turning dark. We were lucky to get a taxi right away. The usual exchange involving where we were going, the price, the bartering, and finally the agreement on price took place, and we got in the taxi, off to the Suwannaho Restaurant.

That restaurant catered to the tourist. When we got there, we were met by an usher at the door, and we needed to remove our shoes. This was typical at Thai houses, to remove one's shoes before entering a house in Thailand. There was a very large pile of shoes at the door, and we selected a place where we could find ours easily when we left. I wondered if everybody would find their shoes when they left; I had been told that poor Saudis went to parties and removed their shoes before entering, only to select a better pair when they left the party early.

We were ushered to the upper balcony to watch the show and eat. We were seated on a pillow on the floor at a table about twenty inches high to hold our food. They brought us a very large selection of a Royal Thai meal, which has many different Thai foods on a serving platter, all in their separate dishes for one to try, with an explanation of each. Then that was removed and we were furnished many different Thai desserts in their separate bowls, or fresh fruit.

While we were eating, they started the show. They explained to us the costumes that each person wore and about the dance – what it represented and why they performed it. They were very colorful costumes and the dancers performed very well. After each dance, they brought out the mythical creations and explained them to us, which helped a great deal in understanding the dances.

In general, a Thai princess was kidnapped and held by some bad mythical creation. I tried to take pictures of the interesting costumes and dances. They prayed and a person or a creature was sent to answer their prayer. They saved the princess, and killed or cast out the kidnapper. All this was done to classical Thai music, while the dancers were performing. They explained that each dancer's movement was done in a special way for a reason. Soon the show was over, and we made our way to the shoe pile to find our shoes so we could leave.

The evening had gone by so quickly with the eating, talking, and taking of pictures. As I glanced at my watch, I saw it was after 11:00PM. The afternoon and evening had gone by so quickly. We were planning on going dancing, but it was just too late, as the places closed at 12:00PM. So we decided to go back to the hotel. We found a taxi and headed for the hotel. However, Dow was hungry, so we found a noodle shop along the way and stopped. We decided to take the food back to the hotel room to eat. They packaged it up in small plastic bags and soon we were searching for another taxi to the hotel.

We arrived at the hotel and went to the room. After arriving at the room, Dow unpacked the food and Singha, and we began to eat and talk and joke and all; it was really more like a small party than just a snack. Soon we were tired and took a shower and settled in for the evening – or *morning*.

The soft glow of sunshine brought morning into our room all too quickly. I was up first, shaved, cleaned up, and then got dressed. Then I waited on Dow to get ready. When she was ready, we went to the restaurant downstairs for breakfast. We checked the menu and both had ham and eggs for breakfast. Dow drank coffee and I had tea as we waited for our meals. With breakfast over, Dow had to go to work. Dow was to meet me at the hotel after work. We were to have our last dinner together before I had to return to work tomorrow.

I returned to the hotel room and started to pack my collection of souvenirs and clothes I had managed to buy while I was in Thailand. I came with one suitcase, but I would be returning with two suitcases and the bronze ware. Early the next morning, I had to fly back to work. It seemed that I had collected more than I thought, and while packing and moving my things, I found out just how much stuff I had. I had bought the shirts, a suit, and all kinds of trinkets. I was glad I had to upgrade my flight to first class on Singapore Airlines to make the flight back, so luggage should not be a problem. After finishing packing, I had some extra time. I walked down to the store beside the hotel. As I left the hotel, I passed a couple of Thai ladies; it always amazes me how that they can be so clean and neat without all the things like bathrooms and showers we take for granted.

I picked up some cards to send and waited behind a lady to make my purchase. After she paid for her items, she turned and, seeing me, said, "I am from New York." The odor from her unwashed sweatshirt, her dirty jeans, and uncombed hair and dirty sandaled feet confronted me. She looked like she had just walked out of spending six months in a jungle. "Are you from the United States also?" she questioned.

"Why, yes," I answered her.

"I am on a tour; are you on a tour also?" she inquired of me.

"No, I am just here for a visit."

"I am not busy tonight; perhaps we could go out to dinner?" she said, then added, "You do like Thai food, don't you?"

"Yes, I like Thai food, but I am going out to dinner tonight with a friend, and I leave tomorrow," I told her.

"Well, bring him along," she replied. "I am in a single room in the Ambassador Hotel, room 607, give me a call if you can go," she said. "I would like to talk to another American besides the old group of people that are on my tour."

She and the odor walked out the door. The clerk took the items I had and the Thai baht I handed her to pay for the items. She was so neat and clean and looked and smelled so clean compared to what had just walked out of the store. I thought how some people really missed the boat in cases like this.

I glanced at my watch and it was 1:00PM, and I was thirsty and hungry. I walked down the street and went into a Thai restaurant. The waitress came and seated me and provided me with a menu. I asked for a Singha, and she left to get it while I made my selection from the menu. She returned with my Singha, and I selected the fried noodles and vegetables. She left to get my order as I enjoyed the Singha. Shortly, I was eating my last lunch in Bangkok – for a long time, I was thinking. When I finished eating, I paid for my meal and left.

I walked down the street a little further to a bookstore. I looked through the selection of books the bookstore had and picked up several books to take back with me, as good books are hard to find in Saudi Arabia – at least the books I liked to read on history and adventure. I finally got my selection of books and it was already after 3:00PM, so I went to the cashier to pay for the books. It was a really nice day as I walked down the street to the hotel.

The street sweepers were cleaning the street as I walked past them. They had a collection of medallions that they collected from the street for sale. These were religious medallions from the Buddhist religion. One old man stopped me and showed me a bunch of the medallions and asked me to buy one; only one baht, he said to me. I selected a bronze one and gave him five baht. He bowed with clasp hands and said, "Sawaddi, Khorp khun", thanking me as I walked on down the street.

I made it back to the hotel and went to my room. I finished packing, getting the books I had just bought into my suitcase. Then I took a shower and got dressed. By the time I finished dressing, it was 5:30PM. and time to go to the lobby and meet Dow.

It was interesting to watch the number of people who go through a public place. One gets to see all kinds:

people in a hurry, people taking their time enjoying themselves, people who think they should be a king or some kind of royalty. Then in came Dow, wearing slacks and a reddish orange top. With the waist-long black hair and wide Thai smile, it just made for a nice picture. She came over to me and I could not help but tell her how wonderful she looked. She thanked me and asked what I had done today. I started to tell her, but then said "I will tell you at supper. Shall we get a taxi now?" I asked.

We walked out of the hotel and found one of the little blue Datsun taxis. Dow went through the bartering for the price, and agreed to a price before we got into the taxi. I had forgotten to buy film that day, so we asked the taxi to stop by a store so that I could pick up some film. The Central Department store was on our way, he said, and soon he was pulling into their parking lot. Dow waited in the taxi as I rushed into the store to buy some film.

I soon found the camera section and picked up four rolls of film so I could take some with me, and took the film to the cashier to pay for it. I was given the film in a bag after paying for it. I rushed back to the taxi so we could be on our way. In the taxi, I loaded some film into my camera so it would be ready.

We were going to the tallest building in Bangkok. On the top floor is a steakhouse. The owners raise Angus cattle in northern Thailand and have them butchered for the steakhouse. The traffic was really slow that night, and it seemed like a long time until we arrived at the building. We enjoyed talking, and I told her how I had gone to a bookstore and gotten some books, and about how I had met the lady from New York who was here on vacation. Dow was really surprised that somebody I didn't know would ask me to take her out.

We arrived at the building and the taxi driver let us out at the entrance. We entered the building and went to lobby area where all the elevators were, pushed the elevator button, and waited. As one elevator door opened, we stepped inside. The button on the elevator was marked as to which one to push to go to the restaurant, so we pushed that button and waited. It seemed like a long wait to get to the top. Finally, the door opened as we reached the top of the building. A lady met us as the door opened.

"A table for two?" she asked.

"Yes," came our response to her question. The lady led us to a table by the window, then gave us the menus and asked what we wanted to drink. Dow selected orange juice and I took a Singha because it would be a long time before I would get another one.

The owner had a ranch up north, so the restaurant was decorated in a Western theme with scenes from his ranch. They had Angus cattle painted on the walls, with the roundup and other scenes. There were some whips, branding irons, spurs, cowboy hats, ropes, and other items from the ranch, also on the walls, to add a feeling of being on a ranch. The butchered Angus was brought from northern Thailand to the restaurant daily to be cooked. It was a nice atmosphere in the restaurant and was dimly lit, which provided a nice effect.

The waitress soon returned with our drinks and asked if we were ready to order. We both selected the T-bone steak and all the trimmings.

"Then how do you want it cooked?" she requested.

I asked for mine to be well done, and Dow wanted hers medium rare. She left us to place our order.

While we were drinking and waiting on our dinner, we tried to pick out different sights in Bangkok. We could see the river and the lights on each side, with no lights in the river except on the slow moving barges going up and down. We could see the traffic on the streets with their lights. Because this was the tallest building in Bangkok, we could see for miles around and make out the signs of stores and restaurants we had been to. Dow pointed out signs from different stores to me. All too soon, the waitress came with our orders.

It was a real feast that was brought to us that night, fit for royalty. That was my last supper in Bangkok and it was a really good one. The steak was the best I'd had since I had been to Thailand. The baked potato was good, as was the salad and the vegetables. It was more like a Western restaurant than one you would usually find in Bangkok. We continued to watch out the window as we ate. With the meal finished, I could hardly move, I had eaten so much. I paid and tipped the waitress.

Instead of taking the elevators back to the street, we climbed the stairs, which took us to the roof of the building. On the roof of the building were a Hawaiian show, dance floor, and bar. The band was playing, and people were dancing as we entered. We were seated at a table where we could watch the show. We both ordered the club's special drink. Then we walked around the rails looking at the night sights of Bangkok we had missed in the stationary window in the restaurant below.

The stars were so bright up there, away from all the lights below. The place had Hawaiian style huts of bamboo on the roof to really add to the atmosphere. Our table was by the railing and gave us a wonderful nighttime view of Bangkok. When we returned to our table, they started playing a nice slow song and we went to the dance floor. The band was good, and when they finished, they started another good song and we stayed on the floor. When that was over, we went to the table and we were ready for drinks. As we sat drinking, I asked Dow, if I were to come back to Thailand in July, whether would she go with me to Singapore.

She thought about it for a while, then asked me "Why do you want to go to Singapore?"

"I want to get some new lens for my Pentax camera I got while in Viet Nam, and other things and to just see Singapore."

She said she would go to Singapore with me. I told her that I would write her and tell her when I would come. I asked her for her address, but Dow is like a lot of Thais and did not have an address, but got her mail through a friend's address, which she gave to me, and I gave her my address. Then it was time for the show, and the performers came out. They had the drums to perform the lighted torch dance. They spun the torches to the beat of the music. It was a really nice show. They did the fire walk and ended the show with a typical Hawaiian dance.

After the show, the band returned and started playing again. An older Thai lady seemed to manage the band and sang. She was not bad on the songs she sang. We danced a couple of more dances. Then I took a 100 baht note and wrote on it, "I am leaving tomorrow, please play "Leaving on a Jet plane" and gave it to the lady. Since they did not know that song, they sang "Silver Wings" for us. They sang as we danced. These two songs became our departing songs since we could usually find somebody that would know one of them. They started, "Silver wings shining in the sunset, silver wings that are taking me away."

As we danced, Dow's long black hair blew in the breeze. When the song ended, we went to the rail to look at the lights with her hair blowing in the breeze. I held her very tight, then we kissed, just as a shooting star crossed in front of us.

"Make a wish," I told Dow, and I knew my wish. When Dow started to tell me what her wish was, I stopped her and told her that her wish would not come true if she told anybody what her wish was. We smiled at each other and returned to the table, ordering another round of drinks. We danced a couple more times, and as we were finishing our drinks, it was closing time, which came all too quickly for us. We headed back to the elevator for the ride down. It seemed to go a lot faster than the ride up. All too soon, we were on the ground floor.

We walked out of the building and went to where the taxis were waiting on people who left the restaurant.

We had the usual bargaining session with the taxi driver then we were on our way.

Going to the hotel, Dow said she was hungry. We made our usual midnight noodle stop at the hawkers on the street. They do a booming business when shows and night clubs let out, as the Thai's all stop to have their noodles before returning home and going to bed. Dow made our selection and we sat down with the taxi driver to have our noodles before returning to the hotel. When we finished, we returned to the little blue Datsun and drove to the hotel.

We arrived at the hotel and made our way to our room. We were both tired and Dow was going with me to the airport to see me off tomorrow. We were soon fast asleep after a very wonderful evening. It was a night to remember for both of us.

Morning came all too quickly. The sun shining in our room woke me. I took a shower and shaved, then finished packing as Dow showered. We went downstairs to have breakfast.

The restaurant was almost empty as we entered to have breakfast. The waitress ushered us to a table and provided us with menus, but we already knew what we wanted. I ordered a couple of orange juices and ham and eggs with coffee and tea. The waitress wrote down our order and left. She returned with our drinks, telling us our breakfast would be ready shortly. We talked for a short time and Dow wondered if I wanted to go to Phuket when I returned. She then told me she had never seen anyone with sunburn and their skin peeling like mine had. She thought that I had some kind of strange disease. I assured her it was only sunburn and nothing to worry about. I hoped I had put her mind at ease. Just then our breakfast arrived. It would be a long time before I would get ham again.

We finished our breakfast and went back to the room. There was just time to pick up my suitcases, as Dow had arranged for a taxi to meet us at the front of the hotel. I checked out of the hotel, giving them the key to our room as we left the hotel. I had already pre-checked out the day before, so I only had to drop off the key. The taxi was waiting on us as we left the hotel. The taxi driver loaded the suitcases and we were off to the airport.

The traffic was not too busy, but it took a long time waiting on all the lights and traffic jams. However, I didn't mind if we were late. Dow and I seemed to have a lot to talk about, each of us telling the other about our childhoods. We talked about me returning in July and going to Singapore, and maybe to Phuket if we have time. We talked about writing each other also.

All too soon, we arrived at the airport. We unloaded and took the suitcases to get in line at the Singapore Airlines counter. It was not long before I was checked in and given my boarding pass. Each thing I did moved me closer to leaving. I realized how lonely I was going to be and how much I was going to miss Dow. We got a drink and they announced my flight, so I had to go check through Immigration. I hugged Dow and gave her a kiss; and I gave her all the baht that I had left over. I had bought a necklace in a shop by the hotel that I gave her. I gave her $100 so she will have money to write to me.

Departures and saying goodbye are a sad time. I walked to Immigration to leave and kept looking back and waving. Dow stayed till I was out of sight in the Immigration Section. I knew why they called this the lonely door now. It may be a happy door when one is coming to meet somebody, but a lonely door when one is leaving somebody behind. I proceeded to the first class lounge and was provided with a drink. In a short time, I was driven to the plane in a car.

The plane was a 747, and I was taken to the upstairs through the winding staircase. I was seated, then it hit me how tired I was. Soon we were backing out of the loading dock area and were on the taxiway to the runway. I had come to Thailand to find a Thai friend I had met in Viet

Nam; instead, I found a new friend, one that I will come back to see again.

The plane reached the runway and the stewardess announced that we should get ready for takeoff. Soon, the plane was speeding down the runway and I was pushed back in my seat, then I could feel the plane leaving the runway. We were on our way to Bahrain. The plane made a turn as I looked out the window and the sights of Bangkok were shinning off the silver wings. It reminded me of the song they sang the night before: "Silver wings are taking me away." As the colored tile roofs reflected the sunshine in my plane window, I settled back for the return to Saudi Arabia.

Chapter 10: Back to Work

As soon as the plane reached cruising altitude, I fell fast asleep. Soon I was awakened to eat. They were serving prime rib – a good meal, but I rushed through it to get back to sleep. Just as I was finishing eating, the stewardess brought a package with a calculator and other items in it. I stowed it and tried to get back to sleep. Finally, I was awakened again with the announcement that we were to be landing in Bahrain shortly. We could see Bahrain as the 747 descended to the runway, then we felt the touchdown, and the brakes on the wheels and motors coming on. We slowed to a reasonable speed, continued to the nearest taxiway, and headed for the terminal. Soon we were veering to the docking area, and then we came to a stop. There was a mad scramble for the passengers to get to the transfer desk to get the Gulf Air flight back to Dhahran from Bahrain. I got in line at the transfer desk and soon had my ticket to Dhahran.

I went to the loading gate area because the flight left one hour after the Singapore Airlines flight came in. It seemed that the returning flyers were not a really happy bunch. They seemed to have been over played and tired out. Many stopped for one last drink before returning to

Dhahran. Soon the boarding began and I got my seat on the return flight. The flight quickly filled up, and the stewardess passed out candy as the plane doors closed and we were off to the taxiway. Then the announcement came on about getting ready for takeoff as we turned onto the runway, and started to make our takeoff. We sped down the runway and lifted off. I only got a quick glance at Bahrain before we were descending to the Dhahran airport. We made our approach and felt some of the weight being transferred to the wheels as we sped along the runway, then the final bump as all the weight was transferred to the wheels, and we were touching down at Dhahran Airport.

    We turned off onto a taxiway, then to the apron to the terminal area. The plane came to a bumpy stop at Dhahran. The plane door was opened and the mad rush to the Immigration area began. Quickly, long lines formed at the counters that were open in the Immigration area. I had my arrival card and had filled it out on the plane. Many rushed to fill out their cards in the line at Immigration. It was soon my turn to give my passport and arrival card to the Immigration officer. He took my passport and never looked up for what seemed like a long time, then he started stamping the passport and the arrival card and handed it back without bothering to look up. I thanked him and he nodded, and I proceeded to get my suitcases and go through customs.

    Each suitcase is handled by hand at the Dhahran airport; I finally found my suitcases and picked them up to go to the lines at customs. I found what I hoped was the quickest line and waited for my turn. Soon it was my turn and I put my suitcases upon the counter. Each suitcase was opened and all the items removed and checked. Then came the hassle of trying to put all the items back into the suitcases and get them closed. The suitcases were marked and I was allowed to proceed at the last gate where the suitcases were checked for the customs mark and then I was allowed to leave the airport.

I went to the exit, but I was grabbed from behind. I turned to quickly see my attacker. "Tony!" I yelled. I was so happy to see a friendly face in the airport. I needed the ride back to camp that Tony would give me. I was glad that I would not have to take a taxi, because the taxis are sometimes kind of questionable. Tony grabbed one suitcase and I took the other as we pushed our way through the crowded terminal where lots of TCNs (Third Country Nationals) were waiting for the return of their friends. Finally, we made it out of the terminal and pushed through the wave of taxi drivers trying to grab your bags to get you into their taxi.

We made it past them and into the parking lot. Several of the cars were double or triple parked, which blocked the traffic flow in the parking lot. We reached the brown pickup that Tony had brought to the airport to pick me up. We threw the suitcases in the back and got into the pickup. It felt good to have made it through the hurdle at the airport. I had known several people that got stuck there for hours. Tony started the pickup and we were inching our way through the parking lot to the highway when the questions started. What was Thailand like? Were the girls pretty? Did they have beer and pork? What was the weather like? Did you find your friend?

I answered the questions the best I could, but some questions only led to more questions. However, it was nice to talk to an old friend again.

We drove slowly down the narrow two-lane road, going through several small villages and towns. Most of the old houses were built out of mud bricks; the poorer people only had tin or cardboard shacks, whereas the newer houses were built from concrete blocks. The tin houses must have been really hot in the summer when the sun hit them. Most of these houses had neither water nor sewage, or electric, except the newer ones. Oil had made this country prosper, but I wished the wealth could help all of its people and not just a select few.

Some of the drivers were not very good or experienced; they honked their horns a lot and put us in dangerous situations. When they wanted to pass, they honked, and if another car was coming, they passed us on the right side while the car going the other way passed the left side. We saw a lot of wrecked cars and Toyota pickups along the side of the road.

We saw head on accidents just off the side of the road and I always wondered how these could happen. Sometimes we'd see a camel coming down the road toward us, only to find out it was kneeling in the back of a Toyota pickup, tied down and transported in the pickup. However, camels often wandered onto the roads and at night they were often hit. Because of the camels' long legs, when a vehicle would hit them, their bodies came back into the windshield and often killed the driver and passengers if the car was going very fast.

We drove in a semicircle because our camp was near Ras Tanura across the bay, so we had to drive around the bay to get to it. The Arabian Gulf and the high humidity made for a lot of unpleasant sticky days working there. Finally, we arrived back at camp and passed the guard at the gate. Tony took me to my room and helped me get my suitcases into the room, then he was off again. It was really nice to be back in my room since I was so tired. I just rested for a moment, then I shaved and got into the shower. Showers have always refreshed me and given me a new lease on life.

Before I went to bed, I thought I would write to Dow just to let her know I made it back all right. I picked up my pen and started to write, and suddenly I felt so lonely after eleven years and having started going out with a woman again. I thought I would have learned a lesson by now. As I was finishing the letter, I thought maybe I should put a little money in the letter for her so she would write back. With all of these things done, I sealed the letter and crawled into bed, thinking the next day I would put in my request for my R&R in July to go see Dow. When I got in bed, I was so tired that I quickly fell to sleep with a smile on my face.

The next day after I got started at work, I got a leave request form. July was the next leave, so I filled in the form and requested the leave for July. Then I made a couple of copies and took one of the copies and wrote a letter on the back of it to send to Dow to let her know that I was planning on returning in July. We could go to Singapore since I would have two weeks, and maybe Phuket if we planned it correctly. I would go to Bangkok and pick up Dow, then we would go to Singapore and spend five or six days, then back to Bangkok for the rest of the leave and maybe Phuket. Boy! I had hardly gotten my feet back on Saudi soil before I was planning on going back to Bangkok!

The school and houses that I was working on could wait. I had to call the travel agent and get a confirmed booking on a flight back to Bangkok. I made the schedule on the Singapore Airline flight leaving on July 2.

The school I was working on was really a mess. It was started by somebody else who had put no planning into it. Management reassigned another person to the project while I was on leave for two weeks. However, during the two weeks I was gone, the project slipped behind 3 weeks. If they would have only followed the schedule I had made and left for them to follow, there would not be a problem; but they had put up steel where equipment needed to be moved in, so it would have to be removed. In two weeks, the only thing that was accomplished was a portable toilet was set on the second floor. The toilet on the second floor had to be removed so the building could proceed with the decking and other work.

Slowly, I started to gather enough information to start making a new schedule. The major problem was the materials. The schedule would show how the materials would impact the project if they were not received when needed. The school was supposed to be finished in August in time for the students to start the new school year. It seemed to take forever to fit the materials into the time frame to do the work after they arrived. All of this was done by hand and you needed all of the shipping and receiving dates.

You only had two known factors in the schedule: how much you had already completed and when they wanted you to finish. I worked on the schedule at work and also took the schedule back to my room to work on it. After a week, I finally had a reasonable schedule. The real question was whether the materials would arrive on time to support the schedule and whether I could get the needed manpower to put in the materials when they did arrive. With the schedule finished, I only had to monitor it to ensure the project was finished on time. Also we could take advantage of doing some things out of sequence to help speed the progress on the project.

I had a meeting with management on the schedule. They wanted to shift manpower and they believed that material would arrive earlier than what is shown. We already had one incident where the Conex container with the needed material to finish some houses was allowed to be cut loose and washed overboard in a storm rounding the Cape of Good Hope on the southern tip of Africa. We were able to shift material scheduled for other houses to complete the current houses, but since we were only building one school, there was no chance of shifting material from another building. With the schedule in place, the race began to finish the school on time.

Mail call became a more important event in those days. I hoped see a letter with a Thai stamp from Dow. Slowly my leave plans were coming together. My leave was scheduled for July 2, 1978. In each of our letters, our plans were coming together. I had sent Dow the copy of my leave request signed for the 2nd of July. That way, she could make some plans also.

Time seemed to drag by; May was over and we were into June. The school was making good progress, but we had some serious material shortages. We were still on schedule but had entered into the critical time of needing material to keep up the progress. We were having trouble clearing material through the port, and the three week wait for some material had turned into six or eight weeks to clear through customs at the port.

The Muslim Saturday and Sunday was Thursday and Friday. Saturday was the first day of work in their week and Sunday was just another workday for them. Finally, one Friday I was off work and got a chance to go into Al-Khobar and do some shopping. It was nice to have a day off, as I had been working every day to keep the school on schedule. I got a ride into Al-Khobar.

The shops closed for each prayer time, since the Muslims pray five times each day. The times kept changing and were posted so they knew when to pray; they must face Mecca when they pray, so all of the prayer shelters and mosques faced Mecca. Religion got really serious during the two major holidays of Haij and Ramadan for the Muslims.

I went to the shops and started looking. I found two Seiko watches, one for Mom and one for Dad, which I purchased to bring back to them. I went to the International Book store to see whether they had any new books, I managed to find one by Thor Heyerdahl called The Tigris Expedition I thought I would like, and I decided that I would get a bible also, maybe to give to Dow.

Then I passed the gold shops and went in, wondering what I could get for Dow. I didn't know her ring size so I would not be able to buy her a ring, Why not a gold chain with a gold medallion that has the Saudi seal of crossed swords on it? I selected an 18-inch chain for Dow and got a smaller one for Mom with a smaller medallion, because she was a lot smaller than Dow. Then I was ready to go back to Bangkok next month.

I made a count down calendar to count the days till I returned to Bangkok to see Dow. I had 10 days left on my count down calendar. I was walking around singing, "Well, my bag is packed and I am ready to go".

I proceeded to the school since we had made a lot of progress on the building. I was fighting with management to keep workers on the project to continue progressing. I received a call from the office that the new project manager wanted to talk me in his office. I got in my pickup and headed for the office complex. I found a parking place and got out my schedule, along with the latest ETA of the material for the school and other information I had about personnel. I walked into the office complex and to the project manager's office area, and the male Philippine secretary of the project manager waved for me to go on into the project manager's office.

I was all ready to show the project manager where we were on the project and when we could be expected to complete the project. I entered the project manager's office with all my plans and schedule to answer any question he may have. I took a seat at the conference table in front of his desk. I started to lay out the schedule on the table.

"Ed," the project manager started, "I am well aware of the schedule that you have made and the progress that you have made on the school, but the school needs to open Aug. 7. We are afraid if you go on leave as now scheduled on July 2, the school will fall behind just like it did last time you went on leave. Then we would not be able to make the Aug. 7 opening date for the new school."

"I have already made plans and purchased a ticket for the July 2 leave date that you approved," I informed the project manager. "If we would increase the hours on the school, we could insure that the school would be ready on time."

"I am sure that you will be able to reschedule your flights," the project manager noted. "If it costs you any extra money, you bring the additional cost to me, and I will see you get paid for it and that you are not out any additional money for rescheduling your flight."

"Well, when can I go on leave then?" I questioned the Project manager.

Without any thought he said, "After the school is finished." Then he added, "August 15 should be a good date."

"Do I have to put in another leave request?" I asked the project manger.

"No," he said, "I will just change the date on this request and you can have a copy of it." As he spoke, he marked out the July 2 date and wrote in August 15 and initialed behind the write in. "Give this to the secretary so he can make you a copy, and have him process it for you also." Then he added, "Thanks, Ed, for being so concerned with the project and allowing us to change your leave and have it rescheduled."

I got up and walked out of the office and gave the leave request to the secretary and told him to make me two copies, then waited on him to go get the copies made and return them to me. He returned shortly with the copies and I left the office to go back to the school.

I really felt stunned as I walked back to the pickup. Only ten days left until my leave, then it was cancelled. I quickly regrouped to try to save what I could. I wrote on the back of my cancelled and rescheduled leave request that I would not be coming to Bangkok on July 2 like I had planned. It was now rescheduled to August 15 and I would write more when I got everything rescheduled. I sent this out to Dow and called up the travel agent and tried to get my flight changed to August 15 and the two tickets to Singapore to the 18th of August.

All I needed now was the confirmation back from the travel agent, then I would send everything to Dow again. I wondered if she would ever believe they postponed my leave. I could only hope she would believe me and that she would not be waiting at the airport like we had planned.

The next day the project manager came to the site to review the work. I took him on a tour and explained to him how everything was going. Then he told me he has agreed to increase our hours from ten hours a day to twelve hours a day. I rescheduled everything and the additional hours allowed us to keep the school on schedule. However, the interior doors were not in port yet.

I asked and got permission to make doors so that the school can start. We made doors from the material we had and got all the doors hung. Now everything was ready to go, and the doors arrived. So we proceeded to change out all of the doors one by one. We had to put all of the furniture in the building. We finished changing out all of the doors and got all of the classroom furniture in place. School started on Aug. 7th and we still had cleanup to do. We moved most of the crew over to start work on the new bowling alley.

The project manager came to the site Aug. 7th when school started. Still, there were odds and ends to do, but they were using the school. He asked me to come to his office after lunch. I wondered what he had on mind. After lunch, before returning to the work site, I stopped by the office complex to see what the project manager wanted. I walked into his secretary's office and found he was not yet back from lunch, but the project manger saw me and waved me into his office. He told me he will be leaving and had left a note to the new project manger about my good work. He handed me a copy of the note he had written to the new manager. He looked up to me and said, "I wanted to tell you that I will be leaving and have left a note to the new project manager about your good work." I thanked him and returned to the site.

The next morning, we were back at work at the bowling alley site. I arrived at the bowling alley early to get my safety speech ready. Before the workers started to work, I gave a fifteen-minute safety talk. It was difficult, as I spoke, to stop and let an interpreter interpret what I had said to the Philippine workers. You always had to wonder what was lost in the translation. With the safety talk finished, the workers went to work.

Just then one of the personnel men drove onto the site. Jim Fox came into our crowded office, cluttered with picks, shovels, hammers, and all kinds of construction equipment since we have not gotten our storage shed moved from the school site yet. "The new project manger wants to talk to you and wants me to bring you into his office," Jim tells me with a big smile on his face.

"As soon as I get these workers started, I will be right with you," I told Jim as I completed instructions on what needs to be done. "Now I am ready," I told Jim and walked to my pickup to follow him as we headed for the project manager's office. When we got to the main office building, I needed to turn in my daily report from yesterday and my three-week schedule showing what we had completed the previous week and what we expected to complete in the next two weeks. After turning them over along with some material request, I made my way to the project manager's office. The old project manager had been replaced and the new manager who replaced him had just got into the office today. I entered Joe Proctor's office with the personnel man, Jim Fox.

"Ed," he begins, "I need you to change your leave again. I know that you have stayed like they requested before and have finished the school on schedule. What remains is the paperwork to finish the project. We are set next week to get the items for the library. I need you to get them moved in place and get them signed off by the proponent. Will you stay and get this done for us?"

"I have already done what you have asked," I told the project manager "Now you want me to do what the materials men should do, and you want me to change my leave again?"

"Ed, you know we have trouble with the materials people; I think you are the only one that can correct the situation and be able to complete the paperwork on the school," the project manager told me.

"I don't know if I will be able to change my round trip tickets again," I explained to him.

"You go get your tickets and I will have our people change them for you," he told me. "What date can I go for sure this time?" I questioned the project manager.

"August 30th you can go for sure," he said.

"You will give me a memo stating that?" I asked the project manager.

"Yes, you go get your tickets, and by the time you get back, the memo will be ready for you," the project manager informed me.

"OK, I will go get my tickets and be right back," I informed the project manager.

I walked out of the project manager's office and back to my pickup. I started it up and drove back to the camp. I cleared the gate of the camp and drove to my room. I went in and got my plane tickets, which already had changed stickers on them. I put them into my pocket and returned to the truck. I returned to the manager's office, and when I walk in, the project manager secretary was holding a memo for me. He passed the memo to me and I gave the plane tickets to him.

"When can I pick up the tickets?" I asked the secretary.

"They will be ready tomorrow; you can stop by right before quitting time and pick them up," the secretary informed me.

I went back to the school site. How could I explain to Dow I won't be coming till August 30th now? I had a copy of the memo from the project manager and I wrote a letter on the back of it and rushed to the post office to send it to Dow so she won't go to the airport to pick me up. I wondered if she would ever believe me again.

The next two weeks were really busy; all of the items for the school came in. Daily, I took a load of materials to the school to have them accounted for and signed for. Finally, the last load was taken to the school and signed for. It was August 28th when I had completed all of the paperwork on the school project and turned it into the office. Also, I had redone the schedule on the bowling alley and the number of personnel it needed to be completed by the date they wanted it to be completed. Then Jim Fox came to our office, smiling and happy, and placed an envelope on my desk with my name on it and left without saying anything.

Oh No! I thought, *I think they want to change my leave again*

I opened the envelope and took out the memo and started to read it. It read:

As of August 30th, your employment contract will be cancelled with this company. Since we have not provided you the required 30-day notice, we will pay you for the 30 days. Your bonus on your contract will be prorated to the August 30th ending date.

What a way to end a contract, I thought. *This is how I am rewarded for changing my leave twice and doing all of the extra work without getting paid for it.* What kind of management did we have? I had to look on the bright side, I will be going to see Dow on the 30th of August anyway.

When I returned to camp for lunch, I started trying to get a year's worth of living crammed into a footlocker. I had to get the bronze ware from Thailand, all of my clothes, books, and everything packed into a 16" by 18" by 32" footlocker for shipment to my folks' house in Kansas.

I went back to work and started clearing my desk for the new engineer coming up from Dhahran that will take my place when I leave. His company was replacing the company I worked for and was bring in a company from Dhahran to take over all the sites they had. Upon learning of my leaving, a lot of the people I worked with and for came to say goodbye.

When work was over, I continued my packing. I didn't have time to sell my TV or my refrigerator so I just gave them both to Tony. He could sell or do what he wanted with them. I gave my workers all the extra soap, shampoo, etc., that I had left over. Finally, I have finished packing my footlocker. I packed my suitcase and I was ready for a shower and then to bed.

Morning came really quickly; the bright sun shone in the windows telling everybody a new day was upon us. I took all of my daily reports and schedules and turned them in to the office along with my footlocker with the shipping address. I received my monthly pay and my R&R money in Saudi Riyals. I have to get the riyals exchanged into U.S. dollars to take to Thailand. However, they still did not have the cash for my settlement money. Also, they would not do anything about the round trip ticket that I had bought. I would end up losing the Saudi return part of the ticket because of them. They told me to come back in the afternoon to get my settlement money.

I had to go to Rahima to get the Saudi Riyals turned into American dollars. When this was completed, it was lunchtime. I went back to the camp for lunch. After lunch, I headed back to the office at 2:00PM to get my final settlement. They did not have my final settlement. They told me they would bring it to me at camp. How could I change any Saudi Riyals into dollars if it is too late? I returned to my room to do my last minute things and take my final shower. I went over to the mess hall for my last meal. I said goodbye to everybody after finishing the meal and headed back to my room.

It was 6:30 and I left for the airport at 7:00. There was a knock on my room door and I opened it, and it was Jim Fox with a check for the final settlement instead of the needed cash. I told him it was supposed to be cash. He just shook his shoulders, said you are lucky to get that, and just walked off. Just as Jim was walking away, Tony drove up to take me to the airport. We loaded the suitcase in the back of the pickup, and I threw my carry on onto the front seat and we were ready for the airport. We drove out the camp gate and headed toward the airport.

The Saudis had started working on a divided four-lane highway from Damman/Dhahran into Rahima/Ras Tanura. It would have access only in select locations with overpasses in these locations. It seemed strange to see tower cranes in the middle of the desert working on where the overpasses would be. The contractors must be European since most Americans contractors used the portable cranes that could be moved and had a larger lifting capacity than the tower cranes. Also, dirt work had started in many locations. I thought how this would be a big improvement over the narrow twisting two-lane road that went through all the villages now.

As we wound along the narrow road, it was high tide with a full moon and the seawater came up next to the road. We were nearing the first checkpoint on the road, and I was glad that the traffic was not lined up there. Sometimes, when they had a bank robbery, murder, or something, the traffic was lined up there for hours. Tony turned to me just as he pulls to a stop at the checkpoint and, waved through, said, "Ed, what are your plans?"

"Well Tony," I said, " this was really unexpected, so right now I do not have any plans. I am just going to Bangkok meet Dow, then go home and start working on getting another job."

As we passed through the small village, there were some kids playing in the street. I saw some women in black dress, with their veils that only let their eyes be exposed. The pickup kicked up a lot of dust as it passed where the last sand storm left the sand and dust on the road. We moved on past the village.

When we reached the outskirts of Dhahran, we were stopped at the railroad tracks, and the train that ran from Damman to Riyadh was passing the railroad crossing. As we waited on the train to cross, a car pulled up beside us on the driver's side, then a car pulled up beside us on the passenger side, then another car pulled up beside the car on the driver's side, and yet another car pulled up beside it. So we had five cars in a row along the tracks waiting for the train to pass, with cars piling up behind them. As the train crossed the railroad crossing, it exposed five cars lined up on the other side of the railroad tracks with cars piled up behind them also. Everybody was honking and yelling. Finally, the car beside us managed to get through and that opened a passageway for us. We had just made it through that hurdle and were back on track heading to the airport with no more railroad crossings.

    We made it to the airport and found a parking place. We got the suitcase and carry-on bag and headed for the terminal to check in. The terminal was still the same, crowded and busy. Now every once in a while, the police came and ran out a lot of the TCNs that had no business in the terminal. That seemed to help a little, if they would only stay out of the terminal. They moved to the parking lot and made it a difficult place to get through. Finally, I was back in line at Gulf Air for the flight to Bahrain. I said goodbye to Tony as they took my ticket and my suitcase.

    Soon I had my boarding pass and was directed to immigration. I waited in line again to get the exit and reentry visa stamped by the immigration officer. Finally, it was my turn to give my passport to the immigration officer. I smiled and passed my passport to the officer, where it was stamped, allowing me to proceed to the boarding gate for the Gulf Air flight. As I reached the boarding gate, I had a minute to sit down and think about what had happened in the past couple of days. I could not understand why I was treated so badly by the company.

    Just then, the Gulf Air people arrived at the gate and the line started forming behind me. Some Saudis pushed and elbowed their way to the front of the line just as the gate agent took my boarding pass, and I was let through the gate. Then the mad rush to the plane was on; I finally made it to the plane and got a seat. Then I could relax for a while. Shortly, the stewardess was passing out candy, the door was closed, and the plane was being pushed back. The props on the engines began their speedy, turning motion that would move us down the taxiway to the runway. We arrived at the runway and the announcement was made about takeoff as everybody had their seatbelts fastened and got ready.

We felt the thrust as the plane moved speedily forward down the runway. Soon we were airborne and on our way to Bahrain. It was only a few minutes and we were in our descent to Bahrain. Soon I could see the lights of Bahrain as we made our approach to the runway. We were landing in Bahrain, taxiing up to the terminal and stopping. The airplane door was opened and the rush to the transit terminal began. I was lucky since I had been here before and knew how to get there quickly. I reached the transit desk and only had a couple of people ahead of me. Soon I was passing my plane ticket to the people at the transit desk and was provided with a boarding pass to the Singapore flight to Bangkok.

I had the normal wait in the lounge at Bahrain for the Singapore Airlines flight. Watching the people in this lounge was always a real experience. Soon it was time for boarding my flight and I went to the boarding gate area.

Arriving at the boarding gate area, for the 2:00AM Singapore flight to Bangkok, it was really nice to see the big Boeing 747 at the boarding gate. It seemed like ages until they started the boarding of the flight. I was lucky and got on the plane early. I got my carry on gear stowed and was soon relaxing in the seat as the plane filled with the other passengers. The door was closed and we were pushed back from the boarding gate at the terminal. Then the engines came to life and started moving the plane along the taxiway. We were nearing the runway and heard the announcement about fastening seat belts and having folding trays in the upright and locked position. The plane turned out onto the runway and we could feel the thrust of the engines as it moved us quickly down the runway to the speed that allowed us to be airborne. We were on our way to Bangkok.

Chapter 11:
Return to Bangkok

I leaned back and enjoyed the flight to Bangkok, wondering what I would do after returning to the States. However, now was not the time to worry about things like that. I drifted off to a pleasant sleep. I was wakened by a stewardess serving breakfast before we landed in Bangkok. The question of whether Dow would be at the airport to meet me was still laying heavily on my mind; if not, maybe I could find her at the shop by the Indra Hotel. I had finished my breakfast and the stewardess was picking up the trays, as most people were finished eating.

Not long after the trays were picked up and the duty free cart had gone down the aisle, the plane made a wide sweep to the right and I could see land below. We started to descend and I could feel the plane nosing slowly toward earth. We heard the very much-awaited announcement: "Please fasten your seat belts and put your trays in the upright locked position; we will be landing shortly at Don Muang International Airport in Bangkok."

The tile roofs reflected the sunrays through the plane's windows, seeming to glow in the sunshine as the plane tipped its wings to one side, correcting its approach to the airport. Slowly we descended to the runway and suddenly there was a bump as the tires touched down on the runway. The brakes on the wheels and on the motors slowed us to a reasonable speed as we reached the exit to the taxiway and turned onto the taxiway. We slowly moved down the taxiway to the terminal and we were soon docking at the terminal. The door was opened and the passengers all picked up their carryons and moved to disembark from the plane.

I was hurrying down the long corridor to the immigration counter. I reached the counter early and handed my passport to the immigration officer with the completed entry form. He looked at the hotel I had listed and said, "I would be able to find a cheaper hotel," as he stamped my passport and entry card and passed it back to me. He said, "Have a good visit", as I took my passport and proceed to the baggage section to get my suitcase.

I made my way to the baggage belt that my baggage would come in on. I was happy when I soon spotted my suitcase. With it in hand, I headed to the customs section, and as I neared the officers, I was waved through. I went outside the doors and was in the arrival area.

I started toward the nearest group to the north looking for Dow. I even took time to read all of the signs. I could not find Dow, so I went back through the group one more time – still no Dow.

Well, I guess I could not blame her with the company changing my leave all the time, I thought.

There were a few people waiting at the southern part of the arrival terminal, so I walked down there with a dragging heart because I'd been hoping Dow would meet me at the airport. I guessed Dow had just given up on me returning to her, and I could not blame her. As I neared the exit, a fat guy moved to one side to meet his friend who was in front of me, and then I saw her. She was not excited like I was. I hurried through the exit, dropped my suitcase, and gave her a really big hug and a kiss. It was so nice to find a friendly face in a group of strangers; probably like finally seeing the lighthouse for a ship after a long trip in a storm to find a safe harbor. I was so glad that she came to meet me.

Dow told me she had a taxi and had gotten a room for us at the Prince Hotel. We gathered up my luggage and went to the exit. We happily left the airport hand in hand and walked to the taxi. I followed Dow out of the airport into the hot moist air outside. A major change from the air conditioning we had just left inside the terminal. I was glad to be back in Bangkok and out of the bad situation I experienced at work. We walked past all of the taxi drivers and the hawkers with their wares on our way to the waiting taxi.

When we reached the taxi, the taxi driver jumped out and opened the trunk so he could put my luggage in. He checked to make sure the luggage was secure before closing the trunk, then opened the door to allow Dow and me to enter. He got into the taxi, started it, and pulled out into the traffic headed into Bangkok. We were on our way to the hotel.

Dow had not stopped talking since we met at the airport. She kept telling me how she thought I was not coming back because of all the changes. If Dow only knew what I had gone through to get back to Bangkok; I tried to reassure her it was the people at work who kept changing the departure dates, not me. I didn't think she would ever understand that; I only hoped she believed me.

When we stopped at a light, I reached into my carryon bag and brought out the gold chain with the Saudi medallion on it I had bought for Dow in Thailand. I gave it to Dow and told her it was gold. She looked at it and thought it was brass. I told Dow it was 18 carat gold. Dow was used to 22 or 24 carat gold, which was a lot darker yellow than the 18-carat gold. To finally settle the gold issue, we let the taxi driver look at the gold, and he assured Dow that the chain and medallion were real gold, saying we could give it to him if Dow doesn't want it. With that, Dow was satisfied it was gold. With that settled, we finally pulled into the parking lot of the Prince Hotel.

We stopped in front of the hotel and got out of the taxi. When the driver opened the trunk, the bellboy took my suitcases out. We went to the reception desk and checked into the hotel, and started for our room after telling the bellboy what our room number was. We reached the room with just enough time to open the door as the bellboy arrived. He moved our luggage into the room and checked to ensure that the air conditioning was working before returning to the lobby, and I gave him a tip.

I told Dow I needed to take a shower and clean up before we do anything, then I headed for the shower with a change of clothes from the luggage. I turned on the shower and checked to make sure it was warm before climbing in. The water was soft and felt so good after taking showers in the hard salty water in Ras Tanura. My hair was so soft after shampooing it in the soft water. I finished dressing and was ready for supper.

We were hungry and went downstairs to get a taxi to go for supper. Dow decided she wanted seafood and we were off to the seafood restaurant. The Bangkok traffic did not seem heavy as we made our way to the restaurant. It showered on the way to the restaurant, which seemed to clear the air, and the shower was over by the time we reached the restaurant. The sky was clearing and the weather was returning to normal.

This was a different type of restaurant to me, a nice place to go when not in a hurry. Upon entering the restaurant, we selected the seafood wanted, which was fish, shrimp, and lobster. We waited in line to pay for the seafood items selected and informed them how we wanted the seafood cooked. We ordered drinks while we waited for our seafood to be cooked, settling down with our drinks and giving us time to talk.

I ordered a Singha and Dow ordered orange juice while we waited on our dinner to be cooked. We had time to talk and I asked Dow why they called her Dow when her real name is Poungkeaw. People called me Ed, which is a shortened version of Edwin, which I could understand.

Dow told me that although her actual name is Poungkeaw, it was too long except for most legal and formal occasions, so most Thai took a nick name that was a lot easier for people to say and quicker to use. They just started calling her Dow, which is the Thai word for star. Thais had a different way of saying and writing things sometimes; a person's name may be spelled in two or more different ways in English. It is all right if one knows the person, but if not, it can be very confusing.

Just at that time, the seafood arrived and we began our feast. We had the seafood plus rice and other side dishes to eat. It looked like enough to last for a week. It all tasted so good compared to the camp food I had been forced to eat. We both ate too much since it was so good and fresh and we were eating outdoors, under the stars. The seafood was just taken from the tank, cooked and eaten, not the frozen or the cooler seafood I had been used to. After eating, we just sat, rested, and visited for a while.

When we left the restaurant, I was too full and tired to go out. We were glad we didn't have a long walk to the taxi. We got the taxi and decided to call it a night and return to the hotel. I was ready to turn in since I did not sleep well on the flight. We wobbled our way out to the taxi since we were so full of seafood. We finally managed to get into the taxi and were on our way back to the hotel to get some badly needed rest. We arrived at the hotel just in time for a toilet break, and then to bed for some much needed sleep.

Morning came all too quickly for me. The sun was bright and warming as we woke. We washed, dressed, and were ready to start a new day. I waited on Dow to finish dressing, and we were ready to start our adventure of the day. We made our way downstairs to the restaurant and were seated. The waitress came and asked what drinks we would have.

"I want tea and Dow wants coffee." I responded. She gave us menus to select what we would have for breakfast. Then she left to get our drinks as we made our selections from the menu. I chose the ham and eggs; Dow agreed to that selection. When the waitress returned with our drinks, we placed our breakfast order. The waitress left, we enjoyed our drinks, and talked about our plans for the day.

We decided to go to the snake farm, then to lunch, then do some shopping before returning to the hotel and getting ready to go out to supper, then dancing at Thai Heaven. The waitress returned with the order, and we quickly attacked our food. It seemed our overeating from the night before had subsided and we both were hungry again. It was really nice to be able to sit down and enjoy breakfast without having to hurry off to work afterward. The meal was good; the long absence from pork in Saudi made the meal even better. We topped off the meal with another tea and coffee. With breakfast finished, we left to find a taxi, finding one quickly and were on our way to the snake farm.

The road was beside the klang (canal) and we watched the boats in the klang on our way to the snake farm. Arriving at the snake farm, it seemed a short drive because we enjoyed the different things that we saw along the way.

We joined the line to get our tickets to the snake farm. When our time came, we got our tickets, the price of which was based on nationality. For the Thai's, the price was one tenth of the cost for foreign tourists. I guessed that allowed the Thais to get to see the shows since they could not afford to pay the price that the tourists paid.

With our tickets in hand, we entered the farm. There was a large selection of snakes at the farm. It was really interesting to be able to see them so close up and be safe behind glass. They had a large python they allowed people to have their pictures taken with. We could view the deadly cobras very close and sometimes they would strike at the glass. While we were looking at the different snake eggs, the bell rang to announce the start of the show.

We walked to the show area and found our seats, ready for the show. It started by a large selection of cobras being brought out. The performers sat and played the flute as the cobras raised their heads and unwrapped their hoods, swaying with the flute player and waiting for the time to strike. This was done three or four times with different snakes. Then they brought a large selection of pythons for the audience to view. The last part of the show was the handling and the milking of the snakes to get the venom for the antivenom drugs.

With the show over, we headed for the sales showroom to see what they had for sale. They had snakeskin belts, wallets, purses, boots, shoes, etc. Also, they had mounted cobras in all kinds of different positions. One mount had the cobra with a mongoose – a large selection to choose from. We decided not to purchase any items.

We left the snake farm, found a taxi, and were soon on our way to lunch. Dow directed our taxi driver to a nice Thai restaurant along the roadside. We were soon settled at a patio table overlooking the Thai countryside. The waitress arrived with the menu and took our drink orders; I ordered a Thai beef salad that could only be eaten with a Singha beer. Dow ordered some Thai curry chicken with rice and orange juice. Soon the waitress returned with the orange juice and the Singha for us, then the curry chicken along with the beef salad was brought to us. We enjoyed a nice easy lunch outside on a very enjoyable day. Soon the meal was finished and we were already behind our schedule.

We left to find a taxi and go to the souvenir and jewelry shops to do some shopping. We made our way along the crowded afternoon streets and came to the shopping area we were searching for. Since rubies, sapphires, and other semiprecious stones were mined and cut in Thailand, it was an exceptional value to buy them there. When the taxi stopped, we wandered in and out of the shops and selected a few souvenirs.

The Thais did some really wonderful woodcarvings at a really affordable price. There were teak woodcarvings and also stone carvings. To really get good bargains, we needed to select what we wanted carefully, then bargain with the owner on a price agreeable to both of us, which took time as well as skill. We bought a few items before six o'clock.

We returned to the taxi and headed to the hotel. We needed to shower, dress, and leave for supper. We planned to end up at Thai Heaven. We arrived at the hotel after the normal dangers of the Bangkok traffic. Most drivers were polite and there was not the amount of accidents one would think for people that drive on the wrong side of the road. We got out of the taxi and went to our hotel room. A good shower would relax us and get us going again. We got dressed and were finally ready to go out for supper. We went back downstairs to get a taxi to take us to the restaurant.

Dow wanted to go to a restaurant that specialized in curry and fish. When we reach the taxi, Dow entered and told the driver where to go to find the restaurant. It was the usual warm and humid weather that night. On the way to the restaurant, we passed a building that was on fire. The firefighters were working very hard to put out the fire, and a large crowd was gathering to watch the fire as we edged past the mass of people and the stopped cars. The firefighters put forth their best effort, but just after we passed, the third floor crashed to the ground.

We reached the restaurant and unloaded from the taxi. It was a nice restaurant done in classical Thai house style. Because of the high rainfall in Thailand, the older houses all have very steep roofs, the height of which helped to keep the house cool. The temples and the more costly houses had tile roofs. The less costly places had thatch roofs. We were directed to a table by our waitress, who gave us a menu and took our usual drink orders of orange juice for Dow and a Singha for me. Dow looked through the menu, which was all in Thai, and selected for us. The waitress took the drink order and the food order before leaving. She quickly returned with our drinks.

Over the drinks, we had a pleasant talk about what we had done and seen that day. While we were talking, our meal arrived, which was noodles and curry with fish and a salad. We continued to talk as we ate. I bit into one of the small hot Thai peppers and it brought tears to my eyes and fire to my throat. I tried to stop the burning by drinking my Singha, and I finally got the fire out as we finished eating. I needed no more of the Thai hot peppers that night. I tried the Thai method of stopping the fire by eating a banana, which seemed to help with the burning.

We left the restaurant, with the memory of the hot pepper in my mouth still in my mind, and went back to the taxi. The traffic was very heavy as we drove to Thai Heaven. We saw the normal street scenes as we buzzed along the crowded Bangkok streets. The street vendors were as busy as ever, catering to the needs of the hungry Thais making their way home or to work or whatever the case may have been.

We finally arrived at Thai Heaven and were late. A lot of the shows had already been performed, but we did not really mind We were ushered to a table, gave the waitress our normal drink order, and sat back to watch the show. When the show was over, we got up and started dancing. We seemed to be lost in time as the music stopped, but we continued to dance while everyone looked at us. Finally we realized the music had stopped and returned to our table. We watched the last show. Then we danced till Thai Heaven closed for the evening.

We walked out of Thai Heaven and caught a taxi and started back to the hotel. We made one stop on the way back, at our local noodle stands on the street. Dow made the selection for us, as they spoke only Thai in places like that even if they understood English. It was a nice evening to sit out under the stars and finish off with a bowl of noodles. When we were finished, we went back to the hotel, full and ready for bed. At the hotel, we celebrated with one final drink before turning in for the evening.

The sun's rays penetrated our room as we both awoke to the new day. I shaved, washed, and got dressed, then read the paper while I waited for Dow to finish dressing. When Dow was ready, we went downstairs to the restaurant for breakfast.

The waitress greeted and seated us, providing us with the menu. She took our order for drinks, and returned to the kitchen, as we reviewed the menu for breakfast. Soon the waitress was back with our drinks. We both decided to have the traditional Thai breakfast of rice soup for a change. We gave the waitress the order as she set our drinks on the table. Soon the rice soup was back for us to eat. It was good and a nice change from the normal breakfast we usually had.

After breakfast, we got a taxi and went to the airline office to confirm our flight and tickets to Singapore. With that completed, we went to the nearby Siam Center to look around at some of the shops there. We bought some odds and ends and souvenirs that we found interesting and that were selling at a reasonable price. All too soon, it was lunchtime and we started searching for some place to eat. We found a nice new restaurant at the Siam Center that had a good menu, and we ordered our drinks. The food was spicy and made for a good lunch. After lunch, we continued exploring the shops in the Siam Center. They had some interesting shops and the hours quickly passed by as we walked around. We soon found it was after 6:00 and we needed to catch a taxi back to the hotel. We walked outside to the street and were able to catch a taxi fairly easily.

We went back to the hotel through the busy Bangkok traffic with the collection of items we had bought at the Siam Center. We arrived at the hotel and made our way to our room. We both showered and got dressed and were soon ready to go out for supper. We made our way back downstairs to find a taxi. The taxi took us to a different seafood restaurant and we were seated by a large pond. The waitress brought us menus and some bread. We ordered our drinks and the waitress left to get our drinks as we selected what we wanted to eat. They had a combination seafood platter we ordered.

The waitress left to get our order as we talked about what we had done that day. I tore off a piece of the bread and threw it into the water. We saw the water swirl as a large catfish came to the surface to get the bread. We continued feeding the fish till we ran out of bread and our order arrived. Then we ordered some more bread so we could feed the fish as we ate our meal. It was really wonderful to watch the fish feed as we ate. All too soon, both the fish bread and our meal came to an end. It had been a really enjoyable meal and a really nice experience feeding ourselves and the fish at the same time. With the meal over, we left the restaurant to get our taxi.

We found our taxi and drove to Thai Heaven to watch the shows and dance. We arrived and were greeted by the doorman, who directed us inside to the show area. We were lucky and got the same table we had had the night before. We gave the waitress our drink orders and then wandered out onto the dance floor and did the bump till the next show started. We then returned to the table to watch the show and have our drinks. Soon the time came to close Thai Heaven and we left to catch a taxi outside. We returned to the same noodle cart on our way back to the hotel to end the day. When the noodles were finished, we returned to the hotel to get a good night's sleep.

That day until our flight left for Singapore, we explored different sites around Bangkok like the Grand Palace, The National Museum, Wat Phra Kaew, and we also made a day trip from the Oriental Hotel (made famous by Jim Thompson) by boat to the old capital at Ayutthaya (sacked by the Burmese), then rode a bus back to Bangkok. Wat Arun (temple of Dawn), Wat Indrawiharm (known for the 32 meter standing Buddha image), Temple of the Golden Buddha (with a Buddha statue three meters tall said to be solid gold), the giant swing at Wat Sutat, and Wat Sahet the Golden Mount (with its great view of Bangkok and its 318 spiraling steps to the top) were all sights we enjoyed, as well as the many shopping centers and other attractions. We did tours and shopping during the days and movies, dancing and nightclubs at night. My two-week visa for Thailand was up the next day. We returned to the hotel and packed to catch our flight to Singapore tomorrow.

Chapter 12:
Singapore, Here We Come

We had to catch the early flight to Singapore so we woke early, finished our packing, and went downstairs to eat breakfast at the hotel. I checked out of the hotel while Dow got a taxi to take us to the airport. After eating and checking out, we loaded our bags in the taxi and left for the airport. Traffic was not too heavy since it was early. We arrived at the airport departure section, unloaded our luggage, paid the taxi driver, and proceeded to the check-in counter.

At the check-in counter, there were only two people in front of us. When those people finished checking in, the lady at the check-in counter asked us, "How many bags do you have to check?"

"We have two bags to check," I responded to her question. "Could we have a window seat?" I asked her.

"Yes, I can let you have a window seat," the check-in lady answered. She handed me back our tickets and luggage check tickets and informed us, "You will be boarding at Gate 12 in one hour."

We made our way to the boarding gate, stopping on the way to buy some drinks. We arrived at the boarding gate and sat down. When they called our flight number for boarding, we went to the boarding gate to get our tickets checked and find our way onto the plane. We found our assigned seats and got our carryon luggage stored in just enough time to settle in before the plane was backing away from the boarding gate. Dow took the window seat and was glued to the window watching all the different things. The plane was soon taxiing to the runway. We turned out onto the runway, felt the power thrust, and were pushed back in our seats as the plane took off.

We were in the air on our way to Singapore. The flight to Singapore is not a long one – only about an hour and 20 or 30 minutes, just long enough to get adjusted to the flight. Dow sat by the window and kept looking out, trying to see everything there was to see. We were served lunch on the flight and were impressed by the service we got on the airline. We even liked the unique uniforms the stewardess wore. Soon the lunch items were cleared away and we heard the announcement to prepare for landing in Singapore. Dow continued to be glued to the window, watching our landing.

Soon we felt the bump of the tires on the runway and the brakes coming on to slow our speed. Then we started to taxi to the terminal. We could feel the plane come to a stop as we arrived at the boarding gate. We were soon making our way through the airport to the immigration section. We got our passports stamped by the very efficient immigration officer, then we headed on to claim our baggage. We went to the baggage claim area to get our suitcases, and it was not long before we find them and proceeded to customs. We were quickly cleared by customs and went to the pick up area. The cleanness of the airport was very impressive.

We found our way to the street side and were met by the hotel taxi to take us to our hotel. We enjoyed the taxi ride to our hotel, impressed by the cleanness of Singapore. It seemed that people in Singapore were very strict in their driving habits, smoking habits, and other activities that people in other cultures did not think too much about. We arrived at the hotel and got checked in. It was so late that we decided just to eat supper at the hotel and wander around a little, then get to bed early. After we got settled in to our room, we went back downstairs to the hotel restaurant for supper. We were soon seated and were given the menu to select from.

They had a very good menu, made up mostly of Chinese food. We made our selection and ordered our drinks, and I had to change from my normal choice and order a local beer to go with supper. We were soon served the food and were given extras to go with our meal by the hotel staff. We had tours starting at 8 o'clock in the morning. By the time we finished eating, it was late and we went to our room to shower and to go to sleep.

We awoke early and got dressed for our first full day in Singapore. It started with breakfast in the hotel restaurant. We had just enough time after finishing breakfast to return to our room, brush our teeth, get our cameras, and go back down to the lobby to catch our tour bus. When the tour bus arrived, we boarded it to find mostly Asians on the bus. They were mostly from Japan and Taiwan. We found a seat close to the front of the bus and just got seated as the bus pulled out and we were on our way to tour Singapore.

The tour took us to different sites around town, showing where the British surrendered during World War II and the prison where the Japanese held the British as prisoners of war. We were told the words from the infamous Japanese general who surrendered Singapore back to the British at the end of the Second World War, who said, "this is a hundred years war and you have only won the first part". Soon it was lunchtime and the tour bus took us to a nice, small curbside restaurant. This restaurant had kind of a buffet type of service. However, they come around to your table to serve the main courses.

The cleanness of the city really amazed us. The people from Singapore were heavily fined for any littering. Also they were heavily fined or imprisoned for traffic violations. The saying was, "The other cities of the world sweep their streets, however Singapore mops their streets." Each shop owner is responsible for the sidewalk in front of their store. The people believed that if the outside of the store was not neat and clean, the inside would be the same, and they would not shop there.

With lunch over, we continued the tour. We were taken to one of the overlooks of Singapore's port and the city. It was one of the busiest and best run seaports in the world, a major shipping port between Asia and Europe and a major shipper of containers, providing a major income for Singapore. The population in Singapore was mainly Chinese, but they had many other nationalities. So there was a very wide variety of different nationalities' holidays celebrated in Singapore by the different ethic groups.

When the tour was over, we chose to remain downtown to look around and not return to the hotel. We found it very interesting, including some interesting stores at which we were able to buy some interesting items.

We found a sort of an open-air type restaurant downtown where the vendors rented a booth from the government and the government inspected the stalls to ensure they were clean and the food properly prepared. Each stall specialized in one kind of food or item, so one could go to four or five stalls to get all the items desired for a meal. It was clean and good and the prices really reasonable. One might go to one stall to get drinks, another stall for rice or noodles and different stalls for the toppings desired on the items selected.

When we finished eating supper, we decided to go dancing at one of the local clubs. We flagged down a taxi and had him take us to one of the nightclubs near our hotel. We reached the area where the nightclub was located and got out of the taxi, surprised to find the nightclub was upstairs. We walked upstairs and entered, finding a nice atmosphere. We quickly found a table and just got seated when the waitress arrived at our table to take our orders for drinks. Just at that moment, the band started to play a song we knew. We got up and danced to the song. We were talking and saying it was a long way home for the both of us as the song was playing. The song ended and we returned to our table.

Dow decided to go to the bathroom after we returned to the table. One of the girls there saw me sitting at the table by myself, and she came over and sat down with me. Shortly after the girl sat down, the waitress brought over a drink for the girl. She started talking to me in English, telling me her name and asking my name. Then she asked if I was working in Singapore or just a tourist. Dow returned to the table at that moment. She was very polite to the unwanted stranger, but did not like the idea of the girl sitting at the table with us.

The band started playing another song that we knew and Dow got up and pulled me onto the dance floor, leaving the unwanted girl at our table. Dow gave me a glance, as if to ask why the girl came to our table, but did not say anything. When the song was over, we returned to the table and the girl was still there. We sat down, then danced a couple of more dances, but the girl still remained at our table.

Dow was getting madder and madder all the time. Since it was late, we decided to leave and return to the hotel. However, the girl was still sitting at the table when we left to return to the hotel. We went down the stairs and outside. The air was crisp and pleasant as we flagged down a taxi to return to our hotel.

The streets were not so busy on our way back. It was late when we got to the hotel and made our way to our room, but Dow was hungry. So we ordered some noodles from room service. I showered while Dow ate her noodles.

Then it was Dow's turn to shower before we both fell asleep.

All too soon, it seemed the sun was shining in our room. We woke up, washed, and dressed. Then it was time for us to go downstairs for breakfast. I was really hungry that day for some strange reason. We found a table and were seated when the waitress brought over coffee for Dow and tea for me. We selected the western breakfast of ham and eggs with toast, finishing just in time to catch the tour bus. It had just arrived at the hotel and the driver came into the lobby to pick us up.

The tour took us to different sections of the city we had not seen. We climbed the stairs and rode the tram that overlooked the city and the harbor. The views were very good and we did not realize the morning was gone and it was noon already and time for lunch. The tour took us to a nice restaurant with good food. We were really hungry from climbing all the stairs.

With our noon meal finished, we were taken to the duty free shopping area. The items bought in this section are all duty free from Singapore duty. This area provided a large income for Singapore in jobs and money, as many people from the nearby countries came here to shop. We went to an electronics shop first, where I bought a new lens for my old Pentax camera that I had got in Viet Nam. It had the bayonet-type lens attachment, which had been replaced by the screw-in type attached lens in the newer cameras, but I was still able to find a zoom lens for my camera.

We looked at watches next. I found that Seiko had just brought out a new quartz watch that was more accurate than the Rolex watches. Rolex watches were only for show anyway; they were too expensive to wear. I bought the watch, which I still have, and it keeps very good time. Dow searched through the watches and found a gold Casio watch that she liked. Dow wants everything in gold. I found a new model AM/FM short wave radio cassette player, made by Sanyo, in about the size of a good paperback book. It was small and easy to put into a suitcase and ship, so I got it. Dow selected the normal size Sanyo that had the same features as the small one.

    I looked at the Ambassador fishing reels, but they cost more there than they did in the States, so I did not buy one. We bought all the items before we moved to the other side of the store, which had the clothing. The more items purchased, the larger the discount received at that store. In the clothing store, we found some of the Singapore Airlines stewardess outfits, and Dow bought a couple of these stewardess outfits. She also found some t-shirts and scarves she liked and bought them.

    We continued shopping and looking at different items till it was time to catch the tour bus back to our hotel. It seemed the ride back to the hotel was really quick this time, and we were soon being let off of the bus at our hotel with all of the prizes we had purchased that afternoon. We made our way to our hotel room with all of the packages, and after putting away all our purchases, we were hungry.

    We decided to go back to the same area where we ate the night before with all of the vendor stalls. We freshened up and went downstairs to catch a taxi. We found a taxi fairly easily that time and were soon on our way to the stall area for supper. It did not take the taxi long to reach the area.

    This area seemed to always be busy. I guessed that no matter where one goes in the world, people had to eat. Since the cost of the food and the number of selections was so good there, it attracted a lot of people. This was close to the famous kite hill, which was a manmade hill where people could fly kites, which were an important part of the life of the people there.

    We moved through the stands and selected the different kinds of food we wanted, then got our drinks and were ready to settle down and enjoy our meal. After eating, we look at the different stores in the area and did some shopping. We were both surprised how late it was, and we were both tired. We started looking for a taxi, though it seemed like the later it was, the harder it was to find a taxi. Finally, we were able to find one and returned to the hotel. We were both tired when we reached the hotel, so we took a shower, looked at some of our purchases, and retired for the night.

The sunshine brought in our last full day in Singapore. We got up, washed, and got dressed. We zipped downstairs for our last breakfast in our Singapore hotel. When we reached the restaurant, the waitress saw us and brought coffee for Dow and tea for me. While she was at our table, she took our breakfast orders; we ordered the breakfast special. The waitress left to get our orders.

We were deciding what we would do that day, since we had a free day. Our breakfast was brought to us and we did not realize how hungry we were till we saw the food. We soon had our plates and cups emptied and were ready to find something to do for the day. We returned to our room, brushed our teeth, and then went back downstairs. We just started out walking down the street and we came across an area of street vendors. We looked through the different stalls where they were selling many different items. Dow found some t-shirts she wanted and we purchased them. At another stall, we found some shirts that fit me.

Most of the shirts they made were for the locals, which were all too small for me, but there we found some shirts that I tried on, and they fit. After bargaining for a while, we reached an agreeable price and I bought the shirts. We continued walking and came across a garden area. The flowers in this area were maintained with great care, it was obvious to see. We walked through the area and stopped and take several pictures. I got to try out my new lens (my old Viet Namese camera was actually made Japan, but I purchased it in Viet Nam).

It was lunchtime; the time passed so quickly when one is busy. We searched for and found an outdoor restaurant in the flower garden. We sat down and ordered our lunch in the flower garden. The flowers were so pretty, tended to by very colorful butterflies. It was so pleasant to sit and eat our meal in a place like that. We took more pictures. I had gotten a Kodak 110 camera for Dow that was the first camera with the drop in film. She found lots of things in the garden to take pictures of. It was simple, and I hoped Dow would use and enjoy it. All too soon, our lunch was finished.

We wandered along the garden paths after we finished lunch. We were told it was a spot to which a lot of the people from Singapore came to have picnics and take pictures. It was a really beautiful day with the sun shining, but not a too bright and burning. Even the birds chasing the butterflies and finding seeds among the flowers were so happy, they were singing as they gathered their daily food. It was late and we needed to get back to the hotel. All too soon, we would need to check out and go to the airport to catch our flight back to Bangkok.

We found a taxi to take us back to our hotel. It seemed like we had just walked a short distance from our hotel, but the taxi driver seemed to take forever to get us back to our hotel. When we got back to the hotel, we headed straight to our room, putting all the things we had bought into our suitcases. We showered and changed clothes and decided to go out to one of the famous Chinese restaurants downtown that we had read about for our supper. We returned downstairs to get a taxi to the restaurant, which seemed to waste no time in reaching the restaurant – a good thing since we both were hungry.

The restaurant was a very nice place with large china vases and statues often seen in movies of a Chinese restaurant. Dow wanted to get her picture taken with some of the large vases and other china items at the restaurant. We were met at the entrance by a waitress in the traditional Chinese silk outfit and she looked stunning. She escorted us to a dining area that was semiprivate and separated from the other diners by screens that sat on the floor. Some screens were carved, some inlaid with seashells that seemed to change color as the light reflected differently on them, all with rare wooden frames.

We were served green tea as we made our selections from the menu. Dow wanted some curry rice and we decided on noodles and mushrooms and other things. The waitress returned to take our order. Our teacups were refilled and I asked for one of the local beers while waiting for our order. The meal turned out to be a real feast! All too soon, we were full – long before we made a dent in our order. We had ordered a lot more food than would fit in our stomachs.

We paid and decided to take a short walk to wear down some of our overeating. It was only a short distance to the hotel where the drink "Singapore Sling" was made famous. We walked to the hotel, which was not nearly as colorful as the restaurant we had just left. I guessed the British are not as colorful as the Chinese. The woodwork was really nice though.

We found our way into the bar and each ordered a "Singapore Sling", so we could say we'd had one where they were made famous. The Raffles Hotel was a real landmark in Singapore, made famous when the British had Singapore as a colony to protect their ships sailing through the surrounding waters.

Full from our meals and relaxed from our drinks, we hunted for a cab to return us to our hotel. We soon found one and were taken back to the hotel. Tired from the adventures of the day, the large supper, and the drinks, we wandered tiredly back to our room. This would be our last night in Singapore. When we reached the room, we were too tired and too full for our usual late night noodles snack. We were soon in bed and fast asleep.

The sun woke us to our last day in Singapore. We got up, showered, and dressed. We made our way downstairs to the restaurant and our last breakfast in

Singapore. We were escorted to our table and served tea and coffee. We ordered our breakfast and then talked about our trip to Singapore and the things we had done and seen there. Our breakfast arrived and, although we were overfilled the night before, we still had room for a hearty breakfast. As we left the restaurant, the restaurant owner met us at the door and gave us a gift for eating at his restaurant. He also gave Dow some red roses. I thought this was very nice of the owner and was very much unexpected by us.

We returned to our room to brush our teeth, then completed the packing. With our suitcases full, we went downstairs and checked out of the hotel. The hotel gave us a gift for staying at the hotel as we were leaving and also provided the taxi to take us back to the airport. Our suitcases were soon loaded in the taxi and we left for the short ride to the airport.

Chapter 13:
Bangkok, We Are Back

The ride to the airport seemed shorter than the ride to the hotel when we arrived. There did not seem to be as much traffic so we made good progress and soon arrived at the airport's international terminal. The taxi stopped at the signed unloading area and we got out and got our luggage. We proceeded to the Singapore Airlines check-in counter and waited in a short line. It was always interesting to watch the other people who were checking in, easily telling the tourists who have their souvenirs, the businessmen with their briefcases, and the people who are just traveling between points. It was soon our turn to check in our suitcases and get our boarding passes and the departure gate number.

We proceeded to immigration to get our passports stamped that we were exiting. With that done, we could proceed to the boarding gate. We had only a short time in the boarding gate area before they called for our flight to Bangkok and we were allowed to board the plane. Soon the plane was pulling away from the boarding gate area, moving down the taxiway, and when we turned onto the runway, they announced for all passengers to be seated, fasten seatbelts, and put tray tables up and in the locked position. We could feel the thrust of power as our plane sped down the runway and we could feel the moment when the wheels left the runway and we were airborne.

In a short time, the stewardess was serving lunch on our Bangkok flight. It seemed they had just picked up our lunch trays when it was announced we were on approach into Bangkok International Airport. We did not get the view we'd had on other approaches to the Bangkok airport for some reason. We felt the flaps going down and the landing gear being locked into place, then the bump as the wheels touched the ground. Soon we had moved from the runway to the taxiway to the airport terminal. The plane was loaded with Thais that had been shopping in Singapore because of the selection and the quality of items available there. Many things in Singapore were not available in Thailand, or were in very limited quantities. The plane came to a bumpy stop at the terminal gate.

Soon we were unloading and moving to the Thai immigration section. At immigration, I was given another two-week visa. With my visa stamped in my passport, we moved to the baggage claim area and, finding our luggage, we proceeded to the customs area. We gave the customs agents our customs form and they stopped us. The Thais have a 100% import duty on all items brought into the country for personal use, like on the stereo we had brought back for Dow.

For items that would be taken back out of the country, like my purchases, the duty was not charged. The only items subject to the duty were the Sanyo tape player/stereo we had brought back for Dow. We had no choice but to pay the duty on the stereo. Then we had actually paid for this stereo twice before being released and allowed to proceed through customs. We walked out of the customs area and into the terminal arrival area, finding an opening in the crowd to go outside to the area where the taxis were. We were able to find a taxi without any problem, and soon we were on our way to the hotel.

The ride to the hotel was really different than the ride in the taxi in Singapore. There seemed to be more traffic and a lot more pollution in Bangkok. The taxi crawled slowly along the crowded street as we made our way to the hotel. We arrived at the hotel, and I checked back in and requested them to bring the luggage we had left at the hotel up to our room. Soon our hotel room was full of the baggage we brought from Singapore and the luggage we had stored at the hotel. It was not long before Dow had her new stereo out and was listening to Thai music on it. When we had sorted through all the luggage, we rested a moment. I turned to Dow and asked her, "Dow, would you want to go with me to the States to meet my mother and father?"

Dow thought about it for a long time, then answered, "No, I do not think I want to go to the United States."

"Dow I am going down now to make my plane reservations; if you want to go, I will make reservations for you," I said. "I will be flying to Manila, then to Mexico City, and then into Kansas City."

"No, I do not think I want to go with you," she responded to my question. We went downstairs to catch a taxi to the airline office. I wanted to reconfirm my airline reservations. I was hoping to add Dow to the flight but she did not want to go to the States. We found a taxi and were able to get to the airline office in a short time.

At the travel agent's office, we were able to confirm my tickets. I paid for them, and we also picked up our tickets to go to Phuket because we left the next day.

With our tickets to Phuket, we went to the Siam shopping center to get some last minute items to take with us. When we had finished shopping for our Phuket items, it was late. We decided to just eat supper at the shopping center, since we were already there. We went to a restaurant we had been to before where the food was good.

We entered the restaurant and it was not crowded, so we found a seat by the window with a good view and sat down. Soon the waitress arrived with the menu and we gave her our drink orders: a Singha for me and an orange juice for Dow. The waitress left to get our drinks as we made our selections from the menu. We gave the waitress our order when she returned with our drinks.

We talked about the things we had seen in Singapore and how clean it was. The waitress arrived with our food, and as we ate, we talked about what we wanted to do when we got to Phuket. I wanted to go fishing and snorkeling where I could take some underwater pictures. We finished eating and paid for our meal. Since it was late, we decided to just go back to the hotel and get our suitcases packed, deciding what we would leave there to put back into storage at the hotel. Since we left for Phuket the next day, we would need some time to get the luggage ready.

We went to the street, got a taxi, and headed back to the hotel. When we reached the hotel, it started to rain. We hurried into the hotel with our purchases to try to keep from getting wet, when the very next day we would be going to a place where we *wanted* to get wet. When we got inside, we headed straight for our room. I got the housing for my underwater camera ready, along with my facemask and snorkel, and got them packed. Dow packed the swimsuit she had gotten at the shopping center, along with the other items she needed. We got these all packed in the suitcase to take to Phuket. Then we repacked the suitcase we would be leaving at the hotel.

When it was packed, we called the bellboy to come picks it up and put it back into storage for us again. With the luggage packed, we could rest for a while. It was late when we finished packing, so we decided to just shower and get ready for bed. We talked for a short time before we both fell fast asleep.

Chapter 14: A Trip to Phuket

  Bright sunlight woke us to a clear day after the rain the night before. We got up and prepared for our trip to Phuket after breakfast. We arrived early at the restaurant, found a table, and the waitress brought tea and coffee to us. She took our order of ham and eggs with toast, which was soon brought to our table as we discussed what we needed to do to make our flight. Soon we had finished breakfast. We headed back upstairs to our room to brush our teeth and complete our packing. After that was done, we took the luggage and went back downstairs. I checked out and confirmed our return date with the hotel. We went outside to get a taxi.
  Soon we were in a taxi and on our way to the airport. The traffic was not too bad that early as we made our way to the old terminal that handled all of the domestic flights. We reached the airport and unloaded at the departure area, then found our way to the Thai Airways check-in counter. We seemed to be the first in line, so we checked in, had our baggage checked, and were given our boarding passes. We were told the gate we'd be boarding from and went to that gate, where there was a short wait before they called our flight for boarding. We boarded the

plane, which was a prop plane. Dow wanted some pictures of her boarding the plane, so I took some as she headed for the plane and then some on the ramp, boarding the plane. Soon we were seated, waiting for take off.

They closed the door and gave the usual speech about seatbelts and tray tables as we went down the taxiway to the runway. We turned out onto the runway and the plane locked its brakes, revved the engines, and released the brakes as we started slowly down the runway. We gained speed slowly at first, then when the throttle was pushed forward, we gained speed quickly and were soon airborne.

As we left Bangkok, the flight went over some very nice and colorful areas, but soon the flight was over water. As we leveled out, the stewardess brought us snacks. The plane was not very crowded and Dow moved to the window seat behind me. It was a short flight to Phuket and we were soon descending to land at the Phuket airport. As we made our descent into the Phuket airport, we could see some of the wooded areas. We flew over what looked like banana and coconut plantations on our approach to the airport. The flaps and landing gear came down and we were touching the Phuket runway.

The runway and terminal seemed fairly new. We taxied up to the terminal and the unloading stairs were moved to the plane to allow us to unload. The day was bright and sunny as we unloaded and made our way to the terminal to get our suitcase. We had mostly carryon luggage and quickly found our suitcase and left the airport terminal to find a taxi.

We found a taxi, loaded our luggage, and were ready to go to the hotel. We agreed to the price of the taxi and paid since none of the taxis has meters. However, the taxi driver asked us to wait, then another couple from France crowded into the taxi with us. They also paid the taxi driver their agreed fare. Finally, the taxi was headed for our hotel, we hoped. It was not too long of a drive to the hotel, and when the taxi pulled up, the driver jumped out and ran into the hotel. We were left to get our luggage out by ourselves. We went to the reservation desk to find that the hotel was *also* paying the driver to bring us to the hotel. The taxi driver had been paid three times for bringing us to the hotel: once by me and Dow, once by the French couple, and the third time by the hotel. We complained to the hotel; they were supposed to pick us up at the airport. They told us they did send the taxi to pick us up.

"Then why did he charge us to bring us to your hotel?" we asked. Our complaint did little, but helped get it off our chests. We were not off to a good start in Phuket; things needed to get better. Soon we were checked into the hotel, and we went to our room and left our luggage. We went downstairs to get a tour for the next day, which was a tour of the island. We also scheduled the boat that would take us fishing, and I could go swimming and snorkeling and take some pictures.

Taking the camera, we went for a walk on the beach late in the afternoon. As we walked along the beach, we saw the bamboo huts that guests could stay in. We stopped at one of the bamboo hut bars to get a drink. I had a Singha and Dow had orange juice, and we asked about the huts for rent to stay on the beach, finding that the price was very reasonable. Mostly rented by backpackers, some of the huts had power and bathrooms, while others had only a place to sleep.

We were sitting in the lounge chairs, drinking our drinks, and watching the sun set into the sea. It was a wonderful sight and made for great pictures.

After the sun set, hordes of mosquitoes made their entrance. They were like an attack squadron of dive-bomber fighters. We moved inside, and since it was time for supper, we had a look at the hotel dinner menu. They had a special on lobster for the night. They had something that looked like onion rings and I ordered some of them, along with a salad. We had our drinks refreshed while we waited on our supper. Soon our meal arrived, and I was really surprised to find that what I thought was onion rings turned out to be fried cuttlefish that had been cut cross wise, making a circle that looked like onion rings, then put in a batter like onion rings and fried.

It was a surprise to me when I first tasted them because I was expecting onion rings. However, after trying them, they were really good. By the time we finished our meal, we were ready for bed. We asked what they do for entertainment on the beach at night. We were told if you want to go dancing, to a movie, or shopping, you have to go over the mountain to Phuket City.

We were tired, so we made our way along the beach back to the hotel. The stars were out, so bright and beautiful, and the sound of the waves lapping on the beach made for a wonderful evening walk. The moon had risen, and its glow seemed to follow us on the water, pointing out our path for us. It was even better than the scenes from the movies. We got the feel of the breeze from the sea in our faces and the smell of the salt water. The breeze kept us cool and helped ward off the mosquitoes.

We did not get any mosquito bites while walking along the beach. We stopped under a palm tree on the beach and kissed as the waves lapped softly on the beach. What a wonderful evening! We arrived at the hotel and made our way to our room. We showered to get all the salt and sand from the beach off. It was late and had been a wonderful day! We said good night and soon we were fast asleep.

The sun rising over the mountain behind the hotel shone its light into our room, starting a new day for us. We got up, washed and dressed, and went downstairs. We headed straight to the restaurant for breakfast. The waitress came to provide us menus and take our orders. Dow had the usual coffee and I had tea. The waitress went to get our drinks as we decided what to eat, both deciding to have the traditional Thai breakfast of rice soup. Our breakfast was soon brought to us and we enjoyed it because we were really hungry. With breakfast over, we went to our room, brushed our teeth, and got our cameras. We returned to the hotel lobby to wait for the tour bus to pick us up. The couple with whom we had shared the taxi from the airport was also waiting on the tour bus. They were still complaining about the deal the taxi driver pulled on us.

When the mini bus arrived, we were the last hotel they picked up from, so we were the last ones on the bus. The tour started by driving along the road by the beach and then taking us to a coconut plantation. At the plantation, they had a large group of trained monkeys. The monkeys were trained to climb the coconut trees, select the ripe – large or small, whichever was needed – coconuts, and throw them to the ground. The monkeys were paid in bananas. They also did not have to pay income tax! The monkeys were trained to dance, but to see them dance they had to be paid in bananas. They did not say how the monkeys' *owners* were paid!

We traveled on to a Wat that had a large Buddhist statue. Dow was really impressed by the large statue. She took several pictures of it, and I managed to get one or two pictures. Southern Thailand is where the largest population of Muslim Thais lives. They explained to us about the statue. Then we got back on the bus go to the next stop.

We traveled into Phuket City and caught a ride on a Thai boat. It was the typical Thai boat, long and narrow with an auto engine for a motor. The boat stopped at a Muslim village built on stilts over the water. The village was set in a small sheltered bay out over the water. There were walkways to each of the houses, and all had access to boats by their houses. We were shuttled in to a restaurant for our lunch. Many of those of us who were tourists needed to go to the restroom, which was of course over the water. Since this was a Muslim community, we did not get any pork. They served the food sort of family style where they passed the serving dishes around and one could take whatever was desired. It was all seafood. There were crabs, shrimp, cuttlefish, and many different kinds of fish, and the food was good. After lunch, we could shop at the little craft stores the village people have set up. We bought some of the items they had made from seashells. With lunch and shopping finished, we loaded back onto our Thai boat and headed for our next adventure.

We traveled to James Bond Island. It was the island they used at the end of the movie "The Man with the Golden Gun". The islands in this area were unique, seeming to just rise straight out of the sea. At James Bond Island, there was a short section of beach between two pillar-like rocks that were covered by vegetation. We landed on the beach area at the island, which had nice white sand and water that was so clear. There were several hawkers on the island selling all kinds of things from the movie, from pictures of the island to seashell necklaces, as well as drinks, snacks, and all. We bought a couple of the items from the hawkers, then loaded back on the boat and headed for our next stop.

The boat took us to an island that had large caves, which were home to the birds that made the nests that were used in bird nest soup. The caves were crossed with all kinds of bamboo scaffoldings. The scaffolding does not look like it would support the weight of a person. However, the scaffold was used only by the people who collected the nests for bird nest soup. The nests were glued together by the saliva from the birds. This was what was boiled out of the nest to make the birds' nest soup. We had eaten birds' nest soup and it was good, though not great; it was not what I would say was so very special – the same went for shark fin soup. However, the Chinese thought both of these were really special.

The scaffolding was really flimsy with only one bamboo pole supporting a very large span. The people who collected the nests only weighed about 90 pounds, but still they fell off this scaffolding from 40 to 90 feet, very often to their deaths. The scaffolding was only used maybe once or twice a year; however, it was left in place. After we had seen where the main item for birds' nest soup came from, I did not know if I wanted it any more.

Another attraction in that area was the honey collectors. Bees made their hives in the cracks and crevices in different places in the islands. The people collected the honey from the hives the bees make, using the same type of scaffolding to access these hives. Also, sometimes on their climbs, they fell, sometimes to their death, or were injured and could not work any more. The honey they collected tasted great; however, I wondered if the climbs for honey and the birds' nests were worth the risks these people took. After this last visit, we started back to Phuket city.

It had started to sprinkle as we headed back in the open boat. The boat pilot passed out sheets of plastic to the passengers to try to keep them dry. The sprinkles finally stop. We put away the plastic sheets, which did not work anyway. Before long, we were pulling up to the dock at Phuket City. We unloaded and were met by the minibus driver, who directed us to the mini bus. We were loaded in the mini bus and were expecting to return to the hotel. However, they surprised us, the driver taking us to a statue of two Thai sisters.

These two sisters had rallied the people in this area to resist the invasion of the Burmese. The guide explained to us how Thailand was shaped like an axe, with the sharp part of the axe facing the countries of Laos and Cambodia, where a lot of the invasions came from. However, the back of the axe was where the most serious invasions came from. This was where Burma was located, which destroyed the old capital and several cities in Thailand before being pushed out of the country. The capital was moved to Bangkok on the river where several canals were built. The two sisters were honored by the statues for helping resist the invasion from Burma. After a full day, we were taken back to our hotel. Being the last on the bus meant we were the first off the bus.

We arrived back at the hotel and returned to the beach, checking to see if the boat we had reserved for the following day to take us fishing and snorkeling would be ready. We were assured it would be ready, then we walked back to the hotel. On our way back, we changed our minds and decided to go back to the same hut in which we had eaten supper the previous night, thinking we would eat there again that night. When we got to the hut, we started looking at their menu. I found a salad made with shrimp, like the salad I like with beef, and ordered it to go with our usual order for drinks. Dow selected a seafood curry and I added some fried rice to complete our supper. Full from supper, we walked back the hotel along the beach.

The stars, the sound of the waves on the beach, and the moon all made for a very special evening again. In the moonlight, we could see a couple skinny-dipping by the beach. Because of the shadows from the trees, they did not notice us. We walked on past them, watching them as they enjoyed the evening and were too busy to notice us. We stopped and kissed in the moonlight with the waves lapping on the beach. We arrived at the hotel and they were having a dance. We went up to our room and showered, changed clothes, and returned back downstairs for the dance. We went in to find a table and the waitress came to take our usual order. We listened to the local Thai band play. They played a mixture of Thai and American songs. As our drinks arrived, the band started to play a song we knew and we got up to dance. After several dances and the long day, we were both tired. The band stopped playing at 10:00PM, and we returned to our room to get some sleep. We had to make one stop on our way to our room, as Dow wanted some noodle soup before going to bed. We stopped at the restaurant just as they were closing and got her some.

The sunrays broke into our room as we rose to meet the warming sunshine. We got up, washed, and got dressed.

We went downstairs to the restaurant to get breakfast. We had a western breakfast that morning: ham and eggs and toast. We finished breakfast and went back upstairs to our room to brush our teeth and change into our swimsuits. I grabbed my underwater camera, facemask, and snorkel. We went back downstairs to the lobby and went out to the beach to get our boat. The boat to take us fishing and snorkeling had not arrived when we got to the beach. When they saw us coming, a boy took off running down the beach to the fishing village to get our boat.

We sat down under the palm trees in the shade to wait, and soon we saw a boat coming, which beached in front of us. We walked down to confirm it was our boat. Since no one spoke English, Dow had to talk to them. Finding out it was our boat, we got aboard. We moved off the beach and into a sheltered cove to catch fish; however, we surprised a couple of couples that were nude bathing in the secluded cove, so we moved on down the beach, letting them continue their bathing. We found another good area that looked like it held a promise of catching fish and stopped.

We waited for a while, then started catching some fish. We caught a few fish, then we had a lull. I decided it would be a good time to snorkel and take some pictures. I slid overboard with my camera and facemask and snorkel. I started snorkeling and taking pictures and soon lost all track of time. After snorkeling a while and taking pictures, I swam back to the boat to see how they were doing. As I snorkeled near the boat, I see things floating down from the boat, so I knew they must be chumming for fish. I decided to go ahead and swim up to the boat, not wanting to scare away any fish that they may have chummed to the boat area. As I reached the boat, I lifted my head to see how the fishing was going. Then I saw that what I thought was chum was actually Dow vomiting because she was seasick. I swung aboard the boat and we headed for shore as fast as the boat could go.

When we reached shore, I got Dow a drink to wash out her mouth, then we found her a 7 Up to help settle her stomach. We settled in the shade of the palm trees to stretch out and relax for a while to regain her land legs. Soon Dow was feeling better. Then we walked back to the hotel.

We took showers to get the salt off and we felt a lot better afterward. We went downstairs and got Dow a bowl of rice soup, which helped her unsettled stomach get back to normal. After Dow ate, she felt a lot better, so we made plans to go into Phuket that night. The taxi driver with whom we made plans, wife which was pregnant, and he said he would like to take her along with us if we did not object. We agreed to meet in the hotel lobby at 4:00PM and then head into Phuket City. We spent the time resting and writing post cards till 4:00PM arrived, then we went downstairs to wait on the taxi driver.

The taxi driver and his wife pulled up to the hotel and we got in the taxi with them. We drove along the beach road, then turned inland. As we turned inland, the road became very steep; as we traveled from side to side on the winding road, we could see we were going up a mountain pass between two mountains. We crested out of the mountain pass with large mountains on both sides of us. Then we started the downward travel winding back and forth as we traveled down to Phuket City.

We arrived at a nice restaurant and the taxi driver and his wife let us out at the restaurant. The restaurant was next to the movie theater, where we would be going after we finished eating. After getting out of the taxi, we made our way into the restaurant. We were shown to a table and were provided the menu. We ordered our normal drinks and the waitress went to get our drinks as we made our selections from the menu. Dow ordered crabs and curry rice, and I settled for the grilled shrimp and rice. The waitress returned with our drinks and took our orders. We were talking about the day's adventures and laughing about what I thought was chum when I returned to the boat before finding out what it *really* was, when the waitress returned with our orders.

The seafood was good at this restaurant and we decided that if we returned to Phuket City, we would have to try to remember this restaurant. We almost forgot about the time as we finished our meal and paid for it. We had just enough time to hurry across the street to the movie.

We then ran across the street to the movie theater. Dow selected the seats she wanted to sit in and we paid for them. The usher came, took our tickets, and escorted us to our selected seats. We were not seated long before they started the previews of the coming movies. When the previews were finished, they started to play the Thai national anthem, and everybody rose as they showed pictures of the king, queen, and his mother on the screen. When the national anthem was finished, everybody was seated and the movie started. The movie was a very strange movie about finding a gateway to hell some place in Louisiana. Dow seemed to like the movie; it was in English, but subtitled in Thai and Chinese. When the movie was finished, we walked with the crowd outside.

After a short search, we found the taxi driver on the street close to where he said we would meet him. He had picked the closest parking spot that was open, which we found easily. We got into the taxi and started back to the hotel. We took the same winding road up the mountain pass. When we cleared the mountain pass and started down the other side of the mountain, the city lights disappeared, and we had a wonderful view of the stars and the sea with the moon shining on it.

The stars seemed so bright we could make out every constellation. We could see a few scattered lights from the beach area huts every once in a while, just to remind us there were some other people still living nearby. It was truly a lovers' setting and we made the most of it. All too soon, we reached the beach road and turned toward our hotel. We could hear the waves washing up on the beach as we drove along the beach road. The moon shining on the water was only broken by the never-ending rows of waves. When we got near the hotel, we had the taxi driver stop and let us out on the beach. It was such a wonderful evening we decided to go for a walk on the beach. It was truly a lovers' walk there, even lovelier than in the movies. The waves washing up on the beach, the breeze on our faces, the moonlight in our eyes, all made for a lovely time. That night we had the beach all to ourselves, or at least we thought we did, except for the crabs and other sea creatures. After a nice walk along the beach, we reached our hotel. We stopped under a palm tree to kiss and talk about things that did not make any sense. We wandered up to our room and talked to each other till we were overtaken by sleep.

Chapter 15: Bangkok, Again

The sunrise brought a stream of sunshine into our room and marked the end of our Phuket adventure. We rose, washed, and got dressed. Then we went downstairs to the restaurant. As we entered the restaurant, the waitress brought us a cup of coffee for Dow and tea for me. We gave her our order for breakfast and talked about last night. Our breakfast arrived and we continued to talk about how wonderful the beach had been the night before. We finished our breakfast and returned upstairs to brush our teeth. We did the final packing for our trip back to Bangkok. When we finished packing, we went back downstairs with our luggage and checked out of the hotel. This time we had learned our lesson and got our own taxi to the airport. Our taxi arrived, we loaded our luggage into it, got in and were soon on our way to the airport. We took the beach road and saw one more view, which was very different from the view we'd seen the night before; then we turned inland and were headed for the airport.

We arrived at the Phuket Airport, unloaded our luggage, and went into the small airport. It was impossible to go to the wrong check-in counter because they only had one. We gave them our luggage and tickets and they gave us our boarding passes. There was only one boarding gate so we could not go to the wrong one there, either. How simple it was to only have one of each. The flight from Bangkok had arrived just as we pulled into the airport. The passengers from Bangkok were getting their luggage as we passed through the boarding gate to get our flight back to Bangkok. It was a beautiful day as we boarded the Thai Air flight to Bangkok.

We boarded the flight, found our seats, and waited for the others to complete the boarding. When everybody was aboard the flight, the doors were shut, and safety procedures announced as we taxied out to the runway. We reached the runway and everybody was seated. The prop plane locked its wheels and raced its engines and then released the brakes and we sped down the runway, feeling the tires leaving the runway as we are airborne. We watched the countryside fade as we gained altitude with our flight. All too soon, we were back over the water and we sat back to enjoy the flight and a snack.

After a short, time, we could see land again as we were making our approach into Bangkok. The smaller prop plane seemed to take a different approach into Bangkok than the larger jet planes did. Or maybe it was the same approach, only at a different altitude, where we could see more. We soon heard the announcement that we were approaching Bangkok and to put our tray tables in the upright position and fasten our seat belts. The approach to the runway was very smooth and the touchdown was with out the large bump like some pilots have on landing. We pulled off the runway and were on the taxiway to the airport terminal. We docked at the terminal and the doors were open and we made our way to get our luggage.

It was really nice not to have to go through immigrations and customs at the end of the flight. We found our luggage at the baggage claim area, then made our way to the street side to find a taxi. They had a long line of taxis waiting so it was easy to find one to put our luggage in and go to our hotel. The traffic did not seem as heavy as we made our way to the hotel. The traffic here was a lot different than the traffic in the small town of Phuket City we had just came from. We arrived at the hotel, and unloaded our luggage and watched the taxi driver leave.

We walked into the hotel and I checked in as Dow had the bellboys take care of the luggage. We got our room assigned, and got our luggage, including the luggage we had in storage, brought to our room. We spent the remaining part of the afternoon sorting out our luggage. We were tired from the beach time and flight time of the past week. We were also hungry from all the things we had done today.

We went downstairs and ate at the hotel restaurant. Most people went out for lunch or supper and did not use the hotel restaurant, so it was fairly empty and easy to find a table. The restaurant seemed to only be busy at breakfast. The waitress arrived with the menu and we gave her our normal drink orders. While she got our drinks, we selected from the menu. I decided on the steak – I had eaten so much seafood I needed to have a change – with a baked potato and green salad while Dow went for some curried chicken with rice.

We gave the waitress our order when she returned with the drinks. We talked about the trip to Phuket, how nice and unspoiled it had been, but too many people were starting to go there and would ruin the wonder of the islands. We were soon finished eating and made our way back upstairs. We took showers and just sat around and relaxed for a while before turning in and getting some sleep.

The sunlight through the window announced another day. We got up, did our usual morning clean up, and got dressed. We went for breakfast at the restaurant downstairs. We found a table and the waitress brought us coffee and tea. We ordered pancakes and sausage for breakfast. We finished breakfast, went back upstairs, brushed our teeth, and were ready to start our day. We returned back downstairs and onto the street to find a taxi.

    Bangkok had a lot of taxis and they were easy to find and a real bargain compared to other cities of the world. Normally, people did not have to wait long to find one unless they were in a real hurry, then it seemed like they were never around. We found a taxi very easily that morning and were soon on our way to the tour agent to get my tickets. The streets were not too busy that morning when we pulled up to the travel agent's office. We got out of the taxi and went into the office. The agents all had somebody with them when we entered the office, so we waited till somebody left and were the next in line. The man before us got his tickets, got up and left, and then it was our turn to get my tickets and we went up to the lady's desk. I asked her about my tickets and she searched through her folder file and retrieved them from the folder. The lady saw that there was only one ticket and then turned to me and asked, "Why are you not taking your friend to the States with you?"

    "I asked Dow to go back to the States with me," I answered, "but she does not want to go with me."

    We went to the Siam Center to do some window-shopping and buy a couple of small items. We found a restaurant and ate lunch at it, then went to the Chase Manhattan Bank. At the bank, I set up a monthly allowance from which Dow can draw to support herself. That should help her and free her up from working the long hours in the sewing sweatshop. After that was completed, we went back outside and caught a taxi.

    While in the taxi heading for our hotel, Dow pulled a really big surprise on me. She told me she wanted me to go with her to the small village where her mother, father, and her children live, called Nongkhal. When we returned to the hotel, we set up with Sam the taxi driver to take us out to Dow's village the next morning. We sorted through our luggage again and gathered up extra stuff to deliver to

Dow's parents. We put our unneeded luggage back in storage. We packed only what we would need for a couple of days. We were tired and went back downstairs to eat supper at the hotel restaurant. After we finished eating, we went back to our room and completed what packing we could. Then we showered and talked a while before we went to bed, preparing to get up early tomorrow for our trip to Nongkhal.

Chapter 16:
The Trip to the Village

We got up early to get everything ready for our trip to Nongkhal. We went downstairs to eat our breakfast. Our usual waitress brought us coffee for Dow and tea for me. She took our order of ham, eggs, and toast for breakfast. While we waited for our meal, Dow was telling me the things we needed to get to take to her home. When our meal arrived, we hurried to eat it. When we finished eating, we made a mad run to get a taxi to go to the store to buy this and that to take to her parents. We picked up toys for the children also. We gathered up all the stuff and grabbed a taxi to take us back to the hotel.

We rushed up to our room, brushed our teeth, and finished packing. We gathered all the things we had bought to take to Nongkhal and went back downstairs to the lobby. I checked out of the hotel again and gave them the date we would return. While I was doing that, Sam the taxi driver arrived with his wife, and he and Dow were packing the car. When I came out, the taxi looked like a car filled with Christmas things, or a car fleeing a war zone. We were loaded and ready to leave. We pulled out into the heavy Bangkok traffic, taking the same road I had taken to

Pattaya. The sights were familiar to me since I had been on this road before. When we reached Chonburi, we turned and headed toward Rayong and Chanthburi. The road was two lane and very narrow and curvy. Soon the landscape changed from rice fields to fields of peppers and tapioca. There were orchards of fruit trees of the native fruit. We saw the trees from which latex comes to make rubber. These trees were scored with a V like cut that catches the latex in a cup as the sap runs from the tree. The cuts did not seem to hurt the trees, as they continued to grow even though they had these cuts in their bark. We saw large trees beside the road that seemed to have become shrines. They were covered with flowers, candles, incense, and other items we were used to seeing in the temples and the spirit houses.

We passed strange looking trucks that seemed almost hand made, painted very colorfully. It seemed the two front fenders, hood, and the windshield had came from the Isuzu Company; however, their beds were all hand made of wood by the local people. These trucks were the beasts of burden in Thailand. They seemed to haul everything: rice, people, fill dirt, and any item that came from farms, such as pigs, bananas, oranges, etc. They did not have doors – only a bench seat for the driver and the passengers. This may also have been their way of staying cool in the hot weather. I was told they could import spare parts but not completed trucks without paying the 100% duty. So this may have been the Thais' way of getting around paying the large duty and still getting the trucks needed to do the work.

When we reached Rayong, everybody was hungry and we stopped for lunch at a typical Thai restaurant. It provided the needed rice for the Thais and also for me. I did not like the curry they ate with their rice, so I just had fried rice. We had already traveled over two hours in the overloaded taxi and still had two hours to travel to get to Dow's village of Nongkhal.

After everybody had finished eating and drinking, we got ready to get back on the road. However, Sam decided he needed some extra energy so he also gets a bottle of Two Bulls energy drink. The Thais really believed that helped them; they took it to help them perform better during sex, as well as at work and any other activities in which they thought it would help them perform. As we traveled along, the country became more isolated. The houses were not so elaborate anymore; they were simple, some no more than straw or matted huts, it seemed. We came to some places where the tapioca farmers had put the roots from the tapioca plants in the road to break them up for use. The roads were narrow two lanes, so we had little choice but to run over them. It did not hurt the tires, and maybe it benefited the farmers. Many times, we had to stop for the trucks that had stopped on the road blocking it as they were loading or unloading. The trucks had some massive loads, and when they went up the steep hills, they were only going at a snail's pace. We often did not have a chance to get around them because of the oncoming traffic. This was very interesting, being my first trip to Nongkhal.

When we neared the towns and villages, they had a private bus system, made up of pickups that had a cover over the back of them and two bench seats on each side in the bed of the pickup. These buses drove between the towns and villages and had no scheduled stops; the passengers paid for the distance they traveled. These buses picked up the people that flagged them down. These pickup buses also took the things the people brought to the market or bought from the markets, like chickens, eggs, fruit, meat, and vegetables. They moved the small produce as well as the people. Later, we would take these pickup buses many times from Nongkhal to Chanthburi and back.

We passed a stone quarry and wound down the road to the village. Later we could tell by how much stone had been removed from the quarry as to how much the area had prospered. After a couple of curves, we crossed the river bridge that was on the west edge of Nongkhal. Now we were in Nongkhal. When we reached the school, we turned left and went past a section of small shops. Then we went by a section that had no buildings before coming to a row house that had seven units in it. Dow's parents lived in this row house on the north end. These row houses had one large room for living and sleeping about 4 meters by 7 meters (roughly 12 feet by 21 feet). They had their kitchen and bathroom out back. They got their water from a cistern, which got its water from rain or ground water during the dry season. Showers were taken with water from the cistern using bowl, a bar of soap, and shampoo. I had to have a great deal of respect for these people when I saw them; they had clean clothes and smelled good, not of sweat or of being unwashed.

We stopped at Dow's parents' place, and I met them. Dow's father who was a blacksmith, making and sharpening the hand tools that the farmers brought to him. It was a hard life standing over a hot forge most of the day. Her mother helped him as well as took care of the kids and cooked the meals.

We unloaded Sam's taxi and it was like Christmas time. Dow passed out the things for her parents first, then to the children. We had presents for all of Dow's family. Dow had a younger sister and two younger brothers. They all stayed with her parents as well as Dow's three children. It made for crowded living quarters, but nobody seemed to mind; they all seemed happy and everybody had a part in keeping the place running. When this was finished, it was late and Sam left to find a place for him and his wife to stay for the night. After Sam left, Dow and I walked down the street to a small store to buy some extra treats for the kids and her parents, and also to the market to get what Dow's mother needed for supper. We also bought some extra things; the apples we brought from Bangkok were a real treat in Nongkhal.

Supper was cooked on a charcoal stove out back. The main item for each meal was rice cooked on this stove, in much the same way in which Americans like to eat bread with their meal. They added whatever meat or vegetable they had, cooked or fresh in season. They ate chicken, pork, beef, as well as all kinds of the local vegetables. They went to the market daily to buy whatever meat and vegetables they needed since they did not have a refrigerator to keep food in. This seemed to also be part of their social program, since they could meet and talk to their friends and neighbors at the market. The Thais tried to keep the flies off the meat in the market, since it was not wrapped in plastic and in a refrigerated case like in the States. This must have been what the markets were like in the United States in the late 1800s and early 1900s. They wasted nothing; the purchase was wrapped in old newspaper. However, you knew that the meat was fresh. I wanted a beer to go with my supper and wanted to get one for Dow's father also. They gave Ott, who was 6 years old, the money and he went to buy the beers for us.

After we ate, it was dark. Shower time was a real experience. I had not taken a shower like this since Viet Nam, using a bowl to pour water over me as I used soap to clean myself, then washing it off with more water from the bowl. It was a real change from the hot showers that I was used to. In Viet Nam, a lot of times when it was raining, we just went outside with our soap and shampoo and got a shower. I was not used to the cool water from the cistern but finally managed to get a needed shower.

After supper and the showers, we sat around and talked to Dow's parents. A lot of the children lined up outside the door to look at this strange foreigner with hair on his arms and chest. They wanted to touch to see if it was real. I knew then how the animals in a zoo or park must feel, always being stared at; the kids did everything but feed me peanuts. At first, it did not bother me. Then it became like I was some sort of freak in a sideshow. I was glad when they hung a sheet on ropes between two trees in a nearby empty lot, then set up a movie projector and showed a movie on the sheet to whoever paid to come see the movie. People moved from village to village, showing the movie in a different village every night. They had to run a generator to get the electricity to do that, or find a house that had electric. A lot of the houses did not have electric power.

There was very little power so everybody went to bed early to save from burning the lanterns they used for light. Besides, they needed to get up early to start work. When the sun came up, they could see to return to their work.

Dow had introduced me to her three children. The oldest girl was named Dang (Roungtip), the middle girl was named Bee (Sriwan), and the youngest was a boy named Ott (Chookait). We had brought presents and candy for all. They seemed to share the large teddy bear we had gotten for Bee. We took pictures of Dow's kids and the house of Dow's parents. They would all go into our album. We also gave them some Baht (Thai money) so they could buy whatever they needed.

We were up early with Dow's parents as they fixed their breakfast over the charcoal stove. Dow had provided me a real treat in this remote place; I got toast over the charcoal fire with my breakfast. When breakfast was over, the monks from the nearby Wat came around with their begging bowls, and the Thais lined up to give rice and food to them, which the monks had to eat before noon that day. The monks went from house to house to collect their daily meal with their begging bowls. This was quite an affair; I wondered if the pastors in the United States could live like that. I guessed that the monks knew where their real support came from when they went daily to the village to get their meals.

The children dressed in their uniforms to go to school. The girls wore white blouses and blue skirts, and the boys wore white shirts and blue pants (shorts). It was really impressive to see them at school, lined up saluting the flag. They even looked nice going down the street carrying their briefcases with school work in them.

Sam got to Nongkhal about 10:30 and we loaded up for our return trip to Bangkok. We hoped Dow's parents were a little better off for the things we had given to them. We were soon on the road, crossing the bridge at the edge of Nongkhal and were on our way to Bangkok.

Dow seemed to have gotten quiet as we traveled along on the way back to Bangkok. She seemed to be going through a withdrawal from leaving the village. Before long, we reached Rayong and everybody was ready for lunch. We started looking for a restaurant where we could eat lunch. Sam selected a restaurant and we stopped for lunch. They only had Thai food, so I get some fried noodles while they got rice and several bowls of food to go with it. Soon lunch was over, and we were back on the road to Bangkok. It was late when we reached Bangkok. We arrived at the hotel and got our things out of Sam's taxi, and he and his wife left as we went into the hotel.

I went to the reception desk to check in while Dow gathered up our luggage. They assigned us a room and we went to the room with our luggage. We took a shower, which was very different from the one we had had the night before in Nongkhal. We dressed and decided to go to the restaurant at the hotel, as we were both tired. When we got downstairs, Dow changed her mind; she wanted to go to a restaurant within walking distance of the hotel, which was a nice change from the hotel restaurant. The waitress came and took our drink orders and left us a menu. We celebrated by having a steak dinner while we wondered what was on the menu in Dow's home in Nongkhal that night. We talked about Dow's village at Nongkhal while we ate our dinner. When we finished eating, we realized how tired we were; we paid for our meal and walked back to the hotel and went straight to our room. After talking a short time, we both fell asleep.

Chapter 17: Back at Bangkok

We woke up in the morning to overcast skies and light showers. We got up perform our morning tasks of getting ready, then went downstairs to get breakfast at the restaurant. Once in the restaurant, the waitress brought us a cup of coffee and a cup of tea with the menu. We settled on pancakes and sausage for breakfast and the waitress went to place our order. We talked about Nongkhal till our breakfast came, then our talking continued while we ate breakfast. We finished breakfast, went back upstairs, and brushed our teeth. We returned downstairs to catch a taxi. We seem slow getting around that morning; however, we found a taxi and went to Indra Shopping Center. I picked up some souvenirs to take with me for the people at home. We also looked around a little, then it was lunchtime. We went to a new Thai restaurant that had opened upstairs. We ordered our drinks while we looked at the menu. I selected the fried noodles and Dow had some rice soup and curried chicken. We were chatting about the prices I had paid for some of the souvenirs I had bought while we ate. Dow said she would do a better job of bargaining to get a lower price. We finished lunch and got up and left by the walkway.

We crossed the street using the walkway to get to the other side. I wanted to buy a gold baht chain. We walked along the street until we found a gold shop. We went into the gold shop. Dow's eyes always glowed when she was around gold. They had many lengths of gold chain hanging on the wall. The case in front of us was full of gold rings and bracelets. I wanted the kind of gold chain that had a bar with a chain-like link at each end to hold the ends together. A one baht chain is ½ ounce of gold and that was enough for me. We sorted through the chains till I found one just the right length for me. I liked that one and decided to take it. Then I asked Dow, "Do you want an engagement ring?"

I saw the gleam in her eye when she started to look at the rings. The owner brought us a Singha and an orange juice for us to drink while we looked at the rings. I've always been the type of person that when I find something I like, I buy it, as long as I can afford it. Dow loved to look; she could spend hours looking at something like rings. After what seemed like hours, Dow had finally narrowed her selection down to three rings. She kept trying them on and looking at them, then she was down to two rings. After a very long time, she finally made a selection. It was a white gold ring with three diamonds across the face. I bought it for her for an engagement ring. The owner gave us a box, but Dow decided she wanted to wear the ring. We walked around for a while till we were both hungry again.

We walked across the street to the Indra Hotel and went to their restaurant for supper. We walked in and were soon seated and given menus. We ordered our drinks, making our selection from the menu while the waitress got our drinks. I had pork chops and Dow ordered fish for supper. The waitress admired Dow's new engagement ring when she brought our dinner. The meal was good, Dow was still looking at the ring and talking about it when we finished eating. I paid for the meal and we left the restaurant, having decided to go to the movie playing at the center. It was a Chinese movie in English but subtitled in Thai and Chinese. The movie was good with a lot of action. The actors seemed to be flying around the screen in their ancient Chinese costumes. The movie did not seem to have much of a script, but did have lots of action. When the movie was finished, we made our way to the street but before we could get a taxi, Dow decided she had to have a bowl of noodles before returning to the hotel. We found a noodle shop, which was a good excuse for me to get another Singha. When we were finished, we got a taxi back to our hotel. The streets were really busy, so it took a while to make it to our hotel When we got to our hotel, we went up to our room and showered. Dow wanted to talk about the ring for a while before we fell to sleep.

Sunday morning brought a very sunny day for us to enjoy. This was to be my last full day in Bangkok. We had planned a special evening to celebrate my leaving. We got up, got dressed, and went downstairs to get our breakfast. Our waitress brought our tea and coffee with the menu. We got the ham, eggs, and toast. After breakfast, we went back upstairs to brush our teeth, then we went for a little walk before doing the packing for me to leave tomorrow.

We went downstairs and out the lobby, and were walking past a tour agent when Dow turned to me and said, "I have changed my mind; I want to go with you to the States and meet your mother and father."

"Dow, it is so late I don't know if I can get you a ticket or a visa to go to the States now," I said. We went into the travel agent to see if we could get a ticket for Dow to go with me. We talked to the lady at the desk. She said that she could not help us get a ticket on a flight that left the next day since it was a Sunday. She suggested we go to the airport early and try to get a ticket from the airlines in the morning. I asked her if she had any visa applications to the United States. She said she did not have any applications and the embassy was closed that day, so we could not get one. She did not know any other place where that we could get a U.S. visa application. We left the travel agent's office and caught a taxi to go to the Japan Airlines office. However, they were closed on Sundays. Then we went to the travel agent's office next to the Japan Airlines office to see if we could get Dow a ticket. The travel agent there told us the same thing, that they could not issue a ticket on a flight that left the next morning since it was Sunday. They also suggested we go early to the airport and try to get a ticket from the airlines at the airport.

We had wasted most of the morning without getting Dow a ticket or a visa to the United States. It was time for lunch, so we decided to eat at a nearby restaurant. We entered the restaurant and got seated. The waitress brought us a menu and we ordered drinks. We made our selection from the menu and talked about how we could get Dow an airline tickets to the US. The waitress brought our food and told us about a travel agent that might be able to help us. When we finished eating, we decided to try the travel agent the waitress knew.

We caught a taxi and went to the different travel agent. The lady was pleasant as we explained our need to get Dow a ticket on the Japan Airlines flight tomorrow to Manila. She said she would like to help but she could not get us on a flight that soon. She also suggested we go to the airport early and try to get tickets on the flight. She did not have a visa application for the U.S. It seemed like our only option was to go to the airport early to try to get Dow a ticket.

We dropped our plans for an evening out on the town and found a taxi to get back to the hotel. We put all of my things in one suitcase because if Dow could not get a flight, I would still have to leave because my visa was up. We put all of Dow's things in another suitcase, so if Dow could not make the flight, she could take all of her things back to her apartment in Bangkok. When we were finally finished, it was suppertime.

We went to the restaurant downstairs at the hotel, found a table, and got seated. The waitress brought us the menu and we gave her our drink orders. We ordered steak, baked potato, and a salad for supper. It was not really a happy supper, knowing I was leaving and not having any idea whether Dow was going to get to go with me. We talked about what we were going to do. Dow would take her suitcase with the things she would need with us to the airport. If she could get the flight, everything would be all right. If not, Dow could take her suitcase back to her apartment in Bangkok. As we finished eating, a kind of dark cloud seemed to hang over us. We decided to take one last walk around the hotel area before returning to our room. We stopped at the hotel taxi stand to make sure we could get a taxi at 3:00AM in the morning and were put on the schedule. The night was pleasant, but because of all the lights, we could not see the stars. We returned to our room when we finished our walk, showered, and talked. We fell asleep early because we had a long, hard day the following day.

CHAPTER 18:
THE START OF DOW'S U.S. VISA

We got up at 3:00AM, washed, got dressed, and finished our last minute packing. I went downstairs to check out of the hotel and Dow waited for the bellboy to take our luggage down to the lobby. When I had finished checking out of the hotel, I went to Dow where she was having our suitcases loaded into the taxi we had ordered the day before. When the suitcases were loaded, we moved out into the traffic on our way to the airport. Since there was not a lot of traffic at that time in the morning, we reached the airport earlier than we had planned and went to the Japan Airlines check-in counter to check me in and take my suitcases. Then we started working on Dow's airline ticket. Since Dow did not have a visa for the U.S., I could not buy her a ticket to the U.S. The only option open to us was for me to buy her a round trip ticket to Manila. When we got to Manila, we'd go to the U.S. Embassy and get her a visa to the U.S., then I could buy her a ticket to the States. I bought Dow the needed round trip ticket to Manila.

We had arrived at the airport at 3:45AM, I had been in the Japan Airlines airport office since 4:00AM, and it was now 6:00AM, the scheduled departure time for the flight to Manila. With everything completed, they rushed me to the airline. They had been holding the flight for me and they closed the door after I entered the plane. I looked for my seat and Dow's, finding them just as the plane was backing out of the gate area. I got my carryon stored and got seated by Dow. Dow said, "Where have you been? I have been on the plane for a long time waiting on you." If she had only known what I had to go through to get her on that flight! But that was over, and we now had to start on the U.S. visa when we got to Manila. Soon the plane was taxiing down the taxiway to the runway for takeoff. The usual announcement about seat belts and tray tables and exits and life jackets was given. We turned out onto the runway, feeling the power thrust from the engines as we sped down the runway. The wheels left the ground and we were airborne and on our way to Manila.

    The flight from Bangkok to Manila was not a long flight. Since we were in a jet, the sights out of the windows were quickly gone as we reached our cruising attitude. We were lucky to get breakfast on the flight since we could not get breakfast at the hotel before we left. We thought we would have time to get some breakfast at the airport, but I was in the airline office till the flight time getting Dow's ticket to Manila. Soon the breakfast trays were picked up and we started to make our approach to the Manila airport. Marcus was still in power there and everything seemed to be running all right. We were soon on the landing approach and could see the mountains and some of the small farms as we made our landing at the Manila airport. We taxied up to the gate at the Manila terminal and could feel the stopping bump that signaled we had docked at the gate and we could start unloading from our flight.

    We made our way down the long corridors that led us to the Immigration Area. We waited in line, and when our turn came, I provided our passports to the Immigration officer. He glanced though the passports and stamped them, then returned them to us. We went to the baggage claim area to pick up our luggage. I got a cart and we waited for a short time before our luggage came. When we had our luggage, we could go to the customs area. We came to the customs area and went to the gate designated for people who have nothing to declare. We were stopped at the gate by the customs agent, who requested to see our passports. I gave him our passports and he saw that we were not from the Philippines, so he waved us on through. We walked out into the arrival area of the airport and made our way to where the taxis were. I had a letter to the hotel from one of my workers in Saudi Arabia, so we found a taxi and asked him if he knew where the hotel was. When he said he did, we loaded our luggage into his taxi and were soon headed for our hotel. The traffic was not bad as we drove along the beach for a long time then turned inland into the major part of the city to get to the hotel. Soon we were stopping at the hotel, unloading our luggage from the taxi and having the bellboy put it on a cart to take to our room. I went into the hotel to the reception desk and provided them with the letter from one of my workers. They gave us the keys to our room once we were registered into the hotel.

The bellboy followed us into the elevator with our luggage. We selected the floor that our room was on and soon the elevator door was opening and we went to our room. The bellboy asked for the room key and opened the door for us. We entered the room, and the bellboy followed us and brought in our luggage. We tipped the bellboy as he left our room. Since we were in and had our luggage, we needed to get to the U.S. Embassy to start the process of getting Dow's visa. We got the papers we thought we would need and went back down stairs.

We got a taxi to take us to the American Embassy in Manila, finding that the taxis were a lot more expensive in Manila than in Bangkok and a lot harder to get. Soon the taxi was dropping us off in front of the U.S. Embassy. We then walked down the long pathway to the embassy entrance gate. At the entrance gate, the Philippine guard stopped us. I provided him my U.S. passport to gain access to the embassy. The guard looked at my passport and said, "You are an American?"

"Yes," I answered him back.

"Well, this embassy is for the Philippinos, so I cannot let you enter," the guard replied.

"Can I speak to the Marine guard?" I asked.

"No," came the reply from the guard, "I cannot let you in."

What could we do? I wondered. We went across the street to a phone booth and called the embassy. I told them I was an American citizen and needed to get a visa application, but the guard at the gate would not let us in. I asked if they could have the Marine guard come to the gate so we could get into the embassy and get the visa application. They confirmed that they would send the guard to the gate so we could get in. We said we were just across the street and would walk back to the gate.

We crossed the street again and were stopped by the same guard at the gate, but while we were at the gate, the Marine guard came down and spoke to the Philippine guard, and we were finally able to get into the embassy. We went to the operations area of the embassy, waiting in line for a long time before we were finally provided with the required visa application form. By then, it was so late we decided to go back to the hotel and fill out the application form. We also needed some copies and pictures to attach to the U.S. visa application form. We went back outside the embassy and got a taxi back to our hotel.

I worked on filling out the application form and when it was filled out, I had to go get the pictures and copies needed to be attached to the form. With all of that done, it was late and we were ready for supper. We walked downstairs and out of the hotel and found a nice restaurant just around the corner from the hotel. We went into the restaurant and found a table, and a waitress came to our table with a menu. We had to change our drink orders because of being in a different country; I ordered a local beer and Dow had an orange soda. We both had the pork chops. Soon we were served our meal, and we talked about all of the problems we'd had that day, but we had made it to Manila and had gotten a visa application. We went to a travel agent and gave her my plane tickets and Dow's return ticket to Thailand. We asked her to make reservations for Dow on the same flights I had to the States. If we got Dow's U.S. visa, we would confirm the reservations and pay for the tickets, and she said she would do that. We would go to the embassy early the next day to hopefully finish with the visa. We were tired, so we returned to the hotel. We took showers and then reviewed the visa application one more time to ensure it was filled out correctly. Then we fell asleep.

The sun brought a new sunny day to Manila. We got up, dressed, and got ready to leave the room. We went downstairs and had our breakfast in the hotel restaurant. We had sausage, eggs, and toast with coffee and tea for drinks. When we had finished our breakfast, we went outside and caught a taxi to the US Embassy.

Once in the taxi, we went straight to the American Embassy and walked directly to the entrance gate. There were three people in front of us at the embassy gate waiting for it to open, and before long people started to pile up behind us at the gate. When they opened the gate into the embassy, we were not stopped at the gate like we'd been the day before; instead, the guard allowed us to enter. We went to the reception area where everyone was turning in their papers, and we were the fourth people to turn in our papers. We turned in our visa application to the Philippine receptionist, then went to the waiting area to be called. We heard and saw the first people at the gate called, then the second, then the third people were called. Since we were the fourth people in line, we had expected to be called next. However, they skipped us and called the fifth people in line at the gate. They continued to call others, but did not call us. We talked to some of the people who were waiting and they wondered why we were not called. We walked around the room, waiting to be called. Soon it was lunchtime, and everybody left to go to lunch. We walked across the street and got a pizza for lunch and hurried back to the embassy waiting to be called. The waiting room was almost empty at 3:00, and Dow went across the street and got us some Pepsis. We continued to wait; at 3:45pm, the last person was called. She was a Philippine lady we'd been talking to, since we were the only ones left in the waiting room. That left only us in the waiting room. They started closing at 4:00 when we were still waiting, and finally at 5:00, we were called by an Afro-American about our visa application.

He asked me why I wanted to take Dow to the States. I explained to him that I wanted her to meet my parents who live there. I told him we were talking about getting married, and I had met her parents but she had not been able to meet mine. The man shook his head and said he can understand that. It was nice to meet an understanding person finally after such a long wait and all the troubles we'd had getting this far. Then he said, "I can think of about twenty good reasons why you cannot get a visa."

I did not understand and said, "Twenty reasons?"

"Yes," he answered. "Twenty reasons: that is twenty American dollars for the two entry visas."

"Twenty dollars?" I said. "I can give you that!" And I pulled a twenty-dollar bill from my wallet and gave it to him. He took Dow's passport, the application, and the money and left for a while. He soon returned with Dow's passport with the visa stamped in it and a receipt for the money I had given to him. We had Dow's U.S. visa after a very long wait. The doors to the embassy were locked and we had to get them opened so we could get out. When we got to the gate, it was locked since it was after 6:00PM. They came and opened the gate to the embassy and let us out. We caught a taxi to go back to our hotel, but instead of going into our hotel, we went around the corner to the restaurant to eat and to celebrate. It was after 7:00PM by the time we got to the restaurant.

    We ordered steak and I had a beer to celebrate getting Dow's visa. Finally everything was starting to come together. It was late when I called the travel agent, rather than going there, to confirm that we had Dow's U.S. visa. They told us they needed to see the visa and the reservations would be confirmed after seeing it, then we could pay for the tickets. They would use Dow's return to Thailand ticket as part of the cost of the other ticket to the U.S. I told her that we would come by tomorrow and show her the visa and pick up the tickets since it was so late, then I scheduled a taxi to take us to the airport early on our departure day. Finally, we could settle down to a nice meal. It was time for another beer. This was really the first time in three days we could relax. We really enjoyed the meal, then we went to the club next door and danced till it was late, finally returning to the hotel to shower and get to bed after a very long day. We were really tired and soon we were asleep.

    In the morning, we got up, washed, and dressed. We went downstairs and had breakfast. After breakfast, we headed for the travel agent. We showed them the U.S. visa in Dow's passport, then paid and got the tickets to the States. We were ready to go! We visited the famous World War II sites near Manila during the day and went to the local dance and performances at night, spending the next two days seeing the sights around Manila.

CHAPTER 19:
USA, HERE WE COME

The day came when we started our trip to the U.S. We awoke early and got our final packing done. I went downstairs and checked out of the hotel while Dow guided the bellboys with the suitcases. I finished checking out of the hotel just as Dow arrived with the suitcases. We went out to the waiting taxi and got our suitcases loaded. We were leaving for the airport to start our flight to the States. The trip back to the airport did not take so long since it was early in the morning.

    We arrived at the airport, where I got a cart to put our luggage on as we unloaded it from the taxi. We went into the terminal and got in line to get our boarding passes and luggage checked. We were early and were the first in line. We were given our boarding passes and had our luggage checked through. We went through immigration, had an exit stamped into our passports. With that done, we then had time to find a place to eat breakfast. We found a small shop that was open and were able to get some drinks and an omelet for breakfast. When we were finished, we made our way to the boarding gate. It was not long before the plane started to board. We got aboard, found our seats, and got our carryon cases stored. We settled down for the long flight to Mexico City. It was not long before the plane was backing away from the boarding gate. We heard the usual safety announcements as we taxied down the taxiway to the runway. We reached the runway, the plane turned out onto the runway, and we begin our takeoff. We were pushed back in our seats as the plane made its takeoff on the runway. We felt the wheels leave the ground and we were airborne. We were on our way to the U.S.!

It was a nice flight and the weather was very calm as we sped toward Mexico City – a good flight but a very long one. When we landed, it was dark in Mexico City. We only took our carryon luggage as we left the flight. Since we were checking through immigration with only our carryon luggage, it was easy. We took a taxi to the same hotel that the Japan Airlines personnel stayed in. It was late by the time we got to the hotel. We chose to just eat supper at the hotel. We went to our room, showered, and tried to get a good night's sleep.

In the morning, we got up, cleaned up, and got dressed. We went downstairs and had breakfast at the hotel restaurant. After breakfast, we went for a walk around the hotel. We came to a bazaar that had a lot of clothing and craft items for sale. Dow bought a nice knitted white and red sweater to keep her warm. We found some other things we bought for souvenirs. Soon it was lunchtime and we found a nice restaurant to eat lunch. It had some good tacos and burritos, which we ate, and I also had one of the local beers. When we finished eating, we went back to the hotel and checked out. We got our carryon luggage and found a taxi to take us back to the airport. We liked Mexico City and wished that we could have stayed there longer. I was to meet Bill from work and go on to McAllen, Texas with him, but he could not get off work to meet us. We arrived back at the airport, and since all we had was our carryon luggage, it made it easy. We went to the check-in counter and got our boarding passes and the boarding gate number.

We were processed through immigration and went to the boarding gate, and then we were called to board the flight.

We found our assigned seats then got our carryon luggage stored. It was not long before our flight was being pushed away from the boarding gate. We were taxiing to the runway and got the usual safety announcements as we taxied. We were then turning onto the runway, where the speed of the takeoff pushed us back in our seats and we were soon airborne. We leveled out and they served us a snack. We were soon landing in Dallas.

When we landed in Dallas, we had to go through the U.S. Immigration and Customs. We got back on the flight and continued on to Kansas City. Kansas City did not have a U.S. Customs and Immigration as it was not an International Airport at the time.

We arrived at the Kansas City airport and picked up our luggage. I called Hertz to pick us up, and we went to the airport office and rented a car to drive to Pittsburg, Kansas. Hertz did not have an office in Pittsburg, so we would take the car to the airport at Joplin the following day. We loaded our luggage into the car we rented, got a map on how to get to Highway 69 south of Kansas City and left. It was about a 3- or 4-hour drive from Kansas City to Pittsburg. We got out of Kansas City before 6:00, but it was getting dark before we made it out of the city. We talked about all the things that had gone on in the past few days, getting Dow her US visa, tickets and all. We hoped some day we could look back on this and laugh, but then it was not a laughing matter. We got on Highway 69 south of Kansas City headed to Pittsburg, and before long we arrived. We were both hungry; I was dying for a Sonic foot- long cheese Coney, so we stopped at the Sonic drive-in only a short distance from my parents' house. We ordered the Coneys to go and took them with us to my parents' house. I needed a change from the rice dishes that we had been eating.

It was only a short drive from the Sonic drive-in to my parents' house. Since Dow had changed her mind about coming with me to the States, I had not called my parents to tell them she was going to be with me. I pulled into the driveway and stopped. I went into the house to see if mom and dad had room for us since I had not told them Dow was coming. Mother opened the door for me and I came in and asked if they had room for a friend and they said yes. I told them I had brought a friend with me. "Is that alright?" I asked.

"Sure," mom said, "we have your old room free."

I went out to get Dow and the food from the car. We brought in our carryon luggage and I returned and got the other suitcases. It was getting late for Dad, so after he had met Dow, he went to bed. He seemed very happy that I had a woman with me. We opened the foot-long cheese Coneys to eat at the kitchen table. After opening the coneys, Dow decided she could not eat something like that, so Mom fixed her some leftover pork from the refrigerator. Mom did not seem too impressed with Dow. When we had finished eating, I gave Mom her spoons from Mexico, Philippines, Singapore, and from Thailand. She had a board with spoons from all the States and now from a lot of foreign countries also. It was too late to get out the other items, so I told Mom we were going to bed and would see her in the morning.

Chapter 20: Travel in the USA

The next morning we got up, got dressed, and got reacquainted with my parents. Dad seemed to really take a liking to Dow and told her all the things he wanted her to look at and sort through. Dad went with me to return the rented car to Hertz at the Joplin airport. I drove down, filled the rented car with gas, and dropped it off at Hertz at the airport. I rode back with Dad, and he was asking me all kinds of questions about Dow. Then he came to the question I knew he would get around to asking sooner or later: "Are you going to marry Dow, Ed?"

"I gave her an engagement ring," I told him. "We will look at it some time, or just ask Dow to show it to you."

When we pulled into the driveway, I got out and opened the garage door. Dad told me it was Friday and they had to go to the senior citizens center at 9:00AM and would just leave the car out for that. It was getting close to 9:00AM when we got back, so both Mom and Dad took off to go to their senior citizens meeting. When they left, Dow said she needed some rice. We walked up to the Ramey's grocery store on Broadway, which was about three blocks from the house. When we got to the store, Dow sorted through the choices and found the rice she wanted. She also got some other things she thought she needed. It was October and cool, and Dow was wearing her open sandals and Thailand summer wear and was not prepared for the cool weather. We returned to the house and Dow cooked her rice for dinner. Mom and Dad ate at the senior citizens center.

    I had my Dodge van stored up on blocks at a friend's garage while I was overseas. So I spent the afternoon getting it out of storage. I took it down to get it serviced before I drove it. When that was finished, I got home and Dad had been with Dow going through his collection of china. He had told Dow to pick out the set of dishes she wanted. He seemed so proud of the items they had selected, which they then wrapped and set aside in the attic for Dow to pick up when she returned. I returned with the van serviced just as Dad and Dow were finishing in the attic. We decided to go to Chicken Mary's for supper. Since I had the van out, we drove the van to Chicken Mary's, which was a famous local restaurant for fried chicken. Mom and Dad had come out there quite often so Mom did not have to cook so much. They had a certain time they wanted to go, which was early, when the restaurant first opened before the large crowds came. We met the wishes of my folks and went early. It was Dow's first time to a place like that and she seemed to enjoy it. We talked about what we were going to do. I wanted to do some fishing, then go to Arizona to see my children, Tammy and Eddy, and my sister. Mom said she would like to go with us in the van. We decided to go to Bennett Springs, Missouri, the next day, spend the night, fish the next day, then return to Pittsburg pack and leave the following day for Arizona. Dad decided he did not want to go with us. We drove back to the house and sorted through the things we had got for them in Thailand, Singapore, Philippines, and Mexico. We talked and looked at the pictures we had taken. Then we all went to bed.

The next day was a day of packing and repacking. We packed the clothes and things we would take to Bennett Springs and the clothes we would take when we went to Arizona. I loaded our things in the van we would take to Bennett Springs. Also, I loaded the fishing tackle we would take. When I went to college, I had made fishing rods. I had a fly rod I had made along with an ultra light rod for trout fishing. These have had experience at Bennett Springs. Dow was not too experienced with rods, so we took a Zebco rod and reel for her. I carried my trout fishing tackle in a claymore mine pouch that I had brought back from Viet Nam. After I loaded Mom's suitcase in the van, we were ready to go. We had eaten breakfast before we started to sort out the things and load them in the van. It was almost lunchtime when the blue van pulled out, headed toward Bennett Springs. We stopped at Long John Silver's for our lunch so we could get the taste of fish on our way to catch fish. It was Dow's first experience in this type of fast food place, but she fit right in and was eating with us in no time. When we finished eating, we were off to Bennett Springs.

It was a nice drive to Bennett Springs, which takes about three hours if one hurries; however, we were not in any hurry. We drove to Greenfield, then took the road east of Greenfield then the road north, which was a two-lane road that had a lot of curves and cross bridges and very pretty wooded country with open fields between the wooded areas. Mom was sitting in the seat beside me with her note pad; she made notes on everything, like what time we got to what town and what we had seen, etc. She had been a teacher and had very wonderful handwriting. We all enjoyed the trip and the sights we had seen. Soon we were pulling into Bennett Springs; from the west one crosses the arched bridge over the Niangua River before entering the Bennett Springs area. We turned in as soon as we crossed the bridge, then we crossed a wooden bridge over the water from Bennett Springs, at the point where it met the Niangua

River. We were soon traveling east on the road south of the Bennett Springs. We turned south to go into the camping area and select our campsite for the evening. We found a campsite just north of the shower and bathroom and left our stove and other items on the picnic table to let others know we had taken this site. We went to the office to pay for our camping site and to get our fishing license and trout tags for the next day. With all of that done, we returned to our campsite and fixed our supper on my old Coleman stove. It was enjoyable to eat outside under the stars. We had the lantern for light, but it was turning cool, so I started a fire. The smell of the wood smoke and cool weather made everybody hungry. After supper, we bathed in the bathhouse and were soon ready for bed, as we would have to get up early. Mom and Dow slept in the bed in the back of the van and I slept on the van floor.

    I rose early and started a fire and cooked breakfast of bacon and eggs and made coffee for Mom and Dow. When everybody was up and dressed and had eaten breakfast, we went down to the springs to fish. I had my waders and fished by the culverts. Dow fished just downstream from me. Mom watched from the van, wrote her notes, read, and drank her hot coffee. It was really wonderful to be in America and to feel the pull of the trout on the rods I had made. We moved and fished up in the fly-fishing area after a while. All too soon, we needed to return to Pittsburg. We loaded up our things and were soon back on the road again, having had a wonderful time fishing at Bennett Springs. We arrived late in Pittsburg, and after I unloaded and stored the things from our fishing trip, I went to get pizza for our supper. After supper, I then loaded up the van for our trip to Arizona. We would leave early in the morning.

    Four AM seemed early as we fixed drinks and our breakfast to eat while we traveled to Arizona. We were all ready and the blue van was headed for Arizona. When Dow finished her breakfast, she crawled in the bed in the back of the van and went to sleep. Mom was in the seat beside me with her coffee and notepad making the record of our trip. We started our 1200-mile trip by getting on the Will Rogers Turnpike (Route I-44) in Oklahoma. This went to Tulsa, then we continued on to the Turner Turnpike to Oklahoma City. Then we would take route I-40 on to Flagstaff, Arizona. We made our way through Kansas, stopping for lunch at a town in Oklahoma. We just pulled into a McDonald's and drove through the drive-thru window, got our order and got back on the road again, eating as we traveled. Dow took pictures of things that were different to her as we traveled. After a long day of travel, we were entering the mountain pass just outside of Albuquerque, New Mexico. We drove through the pass and around a corner and the lights of Albuquerque opened up, and it was really a wonderful sight. We had been traveling for fourteen hours; it was dark and we were all hungry. We stopped at a motel in Albuquerque to spend the night and went to a nearby restaurant to eat. After eating, we went back to the motel, showered, and talked about the trip we had made today. Soon we are all asleep.

In the morning, we got up, got dressed, and packed our suitcases back into the van. We went to a nearby restaurant to eat breakfast. Mom had her coffee and toast with ham and eggs. I had the same except I had tea. Dow went with the pancakes and sausage. We were soon finished with breakfast, and Mom and Dow had their coffee to take with them. We loaded up and got in the van after eating and headed for my sister's new house in Phoenix. The air was crisp, cool but not cold – just light jacket weather. The sun was coming up and we got to watch it climb high in the sky as we made our way out of the valley to the hills on the west side of Albuquerque. It was mostly an arid type of landscape as we wound through the valleys and made it out of New Mexico and into Arizona. We passed by the Painted Desert and Meteor Crater as we made our way to Phoenix. By the time we made it to Winslow, we were all hungry and stopped at a restaurant just off the highway for lunch. When we went into the restaurant, there were a lot of native Navajo Indians eating there. We got seated and were given the menu. Dow turned to me and asked, "Where did these people come from?"

Mother and I could hardly keep from laughing when we told her they are native and had been here for a long time. She said they look like Thais to her. I assured her they were Navajo and were here when the white man first came to America, but maybe they did come from Asia. We had the hot roast beef sandwich, we finished and got back on the road to Phoenix. We reached Flagstaff after lunch and turned south on I-17 to Phoenix. We entered the northern edge of Phoenix, turned east, and made our way to Paradise Valley where my sister lived. After a couple of tries, we found the correct turnoff and were soon at my sister's house. Mom had been taking notes all the way; she had the time we entered each town and what she had seen on the way, but she was unable to read the road map to tell her what town we would be coming to.

We had called my sister before we left to tell her we were on our way, so she was expecting us. It was sure nice to see her and her family again. It had been a long time since I had seen them, although we write all the time. After we put our suitcases away, we called my daughter Tammy and my son Eddy and set up a dinner with them the following evening. I had not seen them in a long time. Tammy was just finishing high school and would soon be starting college.

The next morning, Mom, Dow, and I drove the van over to Apache Junction, Arizona, and picked up Tammy and Eddy. Meeting Dow was a real surprise for them. I had not told them I was bringing her to meet them.

It was quite a drive from Paradise Valley to Apache Junction and back. Many things had changed since I had lived there ten years earlier. We had a nice visit; of course, Tammy had become a real young lady and Eddy, an all

American boy. By the time we got back to my sister's, it was almost time for lunch. My sister's two sons were there also, making nine people for lunch that day – enough for a baseball team. That was the last time all nine of us would ever be together at the same time again. It was a nice day and we ate lunch outside on the patio. We talked and played games and took pictures. Soon it was late, and I had to take Tammy and Eddy back to Apache Junction, since they both needed to go to school the next day. Dow had gotten to meet my children now. We got in the van and went back to Apache Junction. The trip was over all too quickly and we were telling Tammy and Eddy goodbye. Then we drove back to my sister's at Paradise Valley. It was late when we got back and we talked for a little while, then we showered and went to bed.

  The next day, we went for a drive around the Phoenix area. We stopped at an Oriental market so Dow could get the things she needed to cook some Thai food for all of us. Dow was really hungry for Thai food. It must have been really hard on my sister to let Dow cook in her kitchen. That night, we had some Thai food. As Dow was busy in the kitchen with my sister fixing supper, Mom was enjoying just watching and talking to them both and not having to work with them. After supper, we talked about our trip back and the problems we had getting Dow's visa because she made up her mind so late. But it had finally worked out with a lot of extra effort. We showered and went to bed. We would be leaving to go back to Pittsburg in the morning, so we needed to pack our things.

  We really hurried to get out to Arizona, so we decided to take our time going back to Pittsburg. In the morning, we had a nice breakfast at my sister's. Mom and Dow had their cups of coffee in the blue van as we headed back to Pittsburg. We took I-17 north from Phoenix to Rimrock, then turned on highway 179 and took it to Sedona and on up through Oak Creek Canyon. We got back on I-17 just south of Flagstaff. At Flagstaff, we took route 89 north to the Grand Canyon. We took pictures and walked on some trails at the Grand Canyon, but Mom soon tired of walking so we left. We continued north on route 89 till we reached route 160 and turned north on that. It led us into Monument Valley, and we spent the night at Kayenta at a Holiday Inn. The valley is where many western movies had been made, and some of the sights were familiar to us from the movies. In the morning, we continued traveling on route 160. The valley was really wonderful.

Before long, we reach the Four Corners area, which is the only place in the United States that four states touch each other. The states are Arizona, New Mexico, Utah, and Colorado. At Four Corners, we stopped and took pictures with Mom. The Navajos were selling silver jewelry at Four Corners while we were there and Dow had to look at that. Dow tried to speak Thai to the lady selling the silver jewelry and was surprised when she could not understand her. She really thought the Navajos were Thai since she thought they looked Oriental. We bought some necklaces and things from the lady Dow tried to talk to. The Navajo lady then told us that because the price for silver has gone up so much, these pieces would be the last jewelry she had that she could sell. This was the time the Hunt brothers tried to corner the market on silver and it almost worked, driving up the price of silver.

We drove into Colorado on route 160, then on to Durango where we changed to Route 550 and headed north. We stopped several times to take pictures at places like Silverton. Mom and Dow did not like going through the mountains. When we got to Montrose, we turned east on Route 50 and drove through Gunnison. The drive between Montrose and Gunnison was very pretty; the river and lake were very nice and we saw all kinds of people fishing. I stopped and talked to one while we got gas at a filling station. *Maybe one day we can come back and fish h*ere, I thought. We continued on Route 50 through Pueblo and stopped at a small town east of Pueblo to eat lunch. When we went in, the waitress came to me while mom and Dow were getting seated and told me that they did not serve Vietnamese. It was useless to try to explain to her that Dow was Thai, not Vietnamese, and that the Thais fought with us against the communists in Viet Nam. I went to where Mom and Dow were seated and tell them their stove was broken and we could not get any hot food there, so we needed to find another restaurant. We found another restaurant just a short distance down the road and ate there.

We continued on Route 50 and passed through Lamar, then in a short time, we were back in Kansas. We drove on through Garden City and to Dodge City where we spent the night. We checked into a motel, found a place to eat, then went back to the motel to shower and get to bed. In the morning, we checked out and ate breakfast at a restaurant nearby the motel. We stopped and looked at some of the monuments in famous Dodge City. Then we took Route 154 to Bucklin, where we picked up Route 54 into Pratt, then went into and through Wichita. East of Wichita, we took Route 96 over to Route 75 south to Route 47 east, then took Route 57 where we again got Route 69 south into Pittsburg. We were all tired when we got home and Dad was very glad to see us again. We ate sandwiches for supper. I only unpacked some of the things from the van before we showered and went to bed.

The next day was clear but cool. I finished unpacking the van from our trip and put away the things from both of the trips. We then went to Joplin and got some items and spent all day there. We returned home tired, and Mom fixed supper and we all sat around talking. Dad took Dow down the basement to show her something that seemed to be a big secret. Then we played cards for a while. Dow was learning to play pitch.

The next day we went to Chetopa to my Uncle's – Mom's brother's – house. When we got to Chetopa, Uncle Frank was ready to go into town to the restaurant and ate lunch. He had a wonderful dog and we all liked it. We then all got back into the van, drove into town, and ate lunch at his favorite restaurant. The food was good and we had good service. Uncle Frank was in a hurry to finish lunch and get back to his house. When we got back to his house, he got out the card table and we had to play pitch till 5:00, when we left to go back to Pittsburg. Uncle Frank loved to play cards. He didn't care if he won or lost; he just loved to play. When we got home, we ate and talked. Then we showered and went to bed.

The next day was Halloween, so we went to the store to make sure we had enough candy for the trick-or-treaters. This would be Dow's first Halloween. We stayed home and passed out candy to the costumed kids as they came and knocked on the door. Dow was amazed at the costumes the trick-or-treaters had. They came in all sizes, but while it was nice to see the small kids out trick or treating, when the college kids came around, it was sort of out of place.

We woke up to the 1st of November. We ate breakfast and talked about Halloween the previous night and all the costumes we had seen. After we had eaten, we were talking about what we were going to do. Then I got a phone call from the company that I worked for. They had a new job assignment for me in the Panama Canal Zone and they wanted me to go next week. They would send my plane tickets to the airport in Joplin and I could pick them up on the day I left. If I wanted to send a footlocker, I would need to get it to the shipper in Joplin within two days, and the company would handle all the paperwork. I would need to have a list of all the items in the locker and their cost. President Jimmy Carter had signed over the Panama Canal to the Panamanian government and we would be working on the first phase of the hand over.

When I hung up, everybody was surprised about my new job assignment. I decided to go to Gibson's Store to buy some rods and reels to put in my footlocker for shipment. Dow went with me and we got two Berkley

Cherrywood 5 feet 6 inch two-piece spinning rods. We also got two Mitchell 300 reels to go with them. (We still have and use these rods and reels, although they have been around the world a few times.) I picked out some fishing tackle to put in the tackle box I would take. I got enough clothes, I hoped, to last me a year, since I did not know what they would have where I was going. Dow bought presents for her children, parents, and her brothers and sister. Then we went back home and packed my footlocker for shipment.

  Dad came down to the basement while we were packing my footlocker. I told Dow that when I got to Panama, I would try to get married status. As soon as I got married status, I would send for her and we could get married. I did not know why we had never thought of getting married in the States. Anyway, I did not think of it. We went down that afternoon and got Dow her return tickets to Thailand; she would leave the day after tomorrow. Then we took the footlocker to Joplin to get it shipped.

  The next day was spent buying things for me and for Dow to take with us and packing our suitcases for leaving. It was a busy time for both of us. We made many trips to the stores to get things, then back again to get other things that we remembered. Finally all things were packed. Mom and Dad wanted to go out to eat supper, so we took them to Spring River Inn, a nice restaurant in what used to be the old Joplin Yacht Club building. We had a good meal, the chicken and dumplings there always having been a favorite of mine. Dow seemed to be getting Americanized, getting her plate and finding whatever she wanted to eat since it was a buffet. I took a departing picture of Mom and Dad with Dow at the restaurant. (This picture still hangs in our house.) When we finished eating, we drove back to Pittsburg. We showered and did some final packing. Then we talked a lot before going to bed.

Early in the morning, we loaded Dow's suitcases in the van. Then I drove up to David's place. David was going with us to take Dow to the airport in Kansas City since he knew the way. Dow crawled into the bed in the back of the van and went back to sleep as we drove up to Kansas City. I talked to Dave to ask whether he thinks Dow and me should get married. David turned to me and said, "Do you love her?"

I answered without hesitation: "Yes."

Then he said, "You should marry her, you have been single long enough."

We soon arrived at the airport and stopped at the airlines Dow was to take to Thailand. I got Dow's suitcases and Dave drove the van over to a parking place. I took Dow inside and we got her boarding pass, seat, and gate assignment. We walked down to the departure gate she was to leave from, holding hands really tightly. We did not seem to notice Dave when he came up alongside us. We waited at the gate till the others started boarding, then I kissed Dow and she hurried off to get aboard the plane, waving to us the whole time till she got to where we were not able to see her anymore. We watched at the window and could see her in the window on the plane. She continued to wave to us till the plane pushed back from the loading area and we couldn't see her anymore. I turned my head away from David, as I did not want him to see the tears rolling down my face from watching Dow leave.

We left the airport with Dave talking and me shaking my head yes or no in response to his questions, as all of a sudden, I really did not feel like talking. It seemed I had just lost something very important to me and I just let it go. I decided next time I would not let her go. I was quiet on the drive back to Pittsburg; it seemed I had just lost my need to talk. When we stopped at Dave's house, I told him I needed to get back home and headed for the folks' house. I knew Dow would not call when she arrived in Bangkok. However, I hoped that she would write.

After a lonely two days, Mom and Dad took me to the airport at Joplin to catch my flight to St. Louis, which went on to Miami. In Miami, I would pick up a Pan Am flight to Panama City, Panama. I went to the duty free shop while in Miami to buy a few things. The cashier did not speak any English. I gave up trying to tell her what I needed and just walked away. I noticed one sign on only one cash register that read "English Spoken Here." *Why in a busy airport like this, in United States, did no one speak English?* I wondered what our country was coming to.

CHAPTER 21:
OUR SEPARATE WAYS

The flight to Panama City was not a long flight and it was nonstop, so I could enjoy myself. I wondered what I would be doing and what the country would be like, as we winged our way there. It was dark as we made our landing in Panama City, Panama. I had a tourist visa since the company did not have time to get the required work visa from the Corps of Engineers for me. We had a smooth landing and were soon taxiing up to the landing gate. When we had docked at the gate, the door was opened and I headed into a new adventure in a different country. I made my way to the immigration section and was surprised to find not one, but two immigration counters – one counter was for Panama and one for United States Immigration at the airport. I went to the Panama Immigration counter and gave them my passport, which they stamped before waving me on. Then I went to the baggage claim area and I found my suitcase. With my suitcase, I went to the Panama Customs "nothing to declare" section and was waved on through. I went outside the customs area into the arrival area of the airport. I had been told someone would meet me there. I looked around and soon found the person who had been the camp manager in Ras Tanura, Saudi Arabia. He was there to meet me, as he had become the business manager on this project. It was good to see the face of somebody I knew in place of a card with my name on it and some stranger.

We carried my suitcases outside to his car in the parking lot. The lot was fairly well lit and it was easy to find his car. We loaded my suitcases into the car and started into town, driving downtown to a hotel in the local area. The business manager took me into the hotel and got the key to my room. He told me they would be around at 8:00AM to pick me up. I made my way to my room, bringing in my suitcases and looking forward to a shower. I looked around the hotel after showering, finding out that my room was set up with a kitchenette in it, but it had no food. I then decided to get some sleep.

The sun woke me and I went downstairs to get some breakfast. Afterward, I went back upstairs to brush my teeth and then back down again to wait for my ride to work. Soon the business manager picked me up. He took me to an empty office on an army base. This was the building we had been given to set up our project offices in. It had one large room up front and a large room in the back with a bathroom in the middle. We sat down and decided how to partition of the front section with a reception area for a secretary at the entrance door. Off of this would be the office of the project manager and the office of the business manager behind his office. Then there would be a room between the business manager and the bathroom for the copy machine. A long hall from behind the secretary's office would lead to the bathroom and the engineering section in the back of the building. The engineering section would have a large room for all of the drawings and samples, and three rooms off of it for the project engineers.

Panama City had a Sears store and a True Value store. I provided our buyer with a list of tools we would need to put in the partitions and a list of materials that we would need. Only the project manager's office would receive nice paneling and other things to give it a nice looking appearance. By the time we had sent the buyer to get the items to start the partitions, it was lunchtime, We went to a nearby army run restaurant to eat lunch. After lunch, we returned to the office, and I start the layout for the partitions and doors for the offices. When the 2x4s and paneling arrived, we started the partitions for the office. I soon learned that from 12:00 or 1:00 till 3:00, many of the stores were closed for siesta, just when it seemed we had forgotten something or were short something.

After work, I was taken back to the hotel by the senior supervisor, with whom I had worked in Khamis in Saudi Arabia. He stopped at a grocery store and I bought some things to fix my meals with back at the hotel. It was lucky I had packed a cooking kit in my footlocker, although it had not arrived yet.

I continued to work to complete the offices and they were soon finished. When the offices were done, we still had no furniture. The company did not want to pay the high cost for desks. They asked me for a suggestion, and I suggest just buying two two-drawer file cabinets, then we would get a hollow wooden door for the desktops. I was told to go ahead and make the desks for the office. I made a very special desk for the office of the project managers. We put paneling on the front and the sides and made a drawer between the file cabinets where their legs would go. We also made a nice one for the reception area. The remaining desks were functional but basic.

It was not long until Thanksgiving came. The whole crew from the project gathered at one of the trailers we had for our Thanksgiving dinner. It was nice and sunny and we ate our turkey and dressing outside on the patio. We were all wondering how they were enjoying their Thanksgiving dinner back in the States, as some states already had snow.

When I first got to Panama I had sent Dow a letter so she would know my new address. It took about two weeks each way for the letters to travel from Panama to Thailand. In the Canal Zone, they had a Chase Manhattan Bank in Balboa. I opened an account there so I could transfer funds from Panama to the account I had for Dow in Bangkok.

We were very busy setting up the projects. The projects were all over in the Panama Canal Zone. Many were small remodeling projects, others were major projects like new post offices in existing buildings and reworking the runways to handle more traffic, etc. The supervision was spread too thin over a wide section; I had as many as ten projects going on at once. I was hard pressed to keep all the projects going because of lack of material and poor workers. It was always hard to go through a new workforce and find a worker who can perform. That always took a lot of time on new projects. It was not like in the States, where I could get ten experienced carpenters from the labor hall.

We were very busy working on all of the projects. I set up a small carpenter shop that turned out the concrete forms and other needed things for the project, like a table for the copy machine and drawing tables for the drafters. I kept busy on all the projects and time went by rather quickly.

Soon we were celebrating Christmas. I had been lucky and was able to get some of the better workers from Ras Tanura, Saudi Arabia brought to our project in Panama. I sent out Christmas gifts to Mom, Dad, and Tammy and Eddy. Tammy had enough credits to graduate from High School early and was ready to start college, so I sent her money to help her start college. The project workers gathered together to have Christmas dinner since we were all away from our families. It was the typical Christmas dinner with both turkey and ham. We ate out on the patio and wondered how many families in the States could eat Christmas dinner outside on their patio.

We celebrated New Year's to mark the end of 1978 and the start of 1979, wondering what things 1979 would bring to us. Work had settled down into a routine by then. We were stretched thin but doing the best we could.

The New Year brought my much-awaited married status. As soon as I got it, I sent Dow a letter asking her to come to Panama and marry me. I did not have a phone number to call her, so I had to wait to see what her answer would be. I sent another letter in case the first one was lost, then I started sending out letters daily. One week went by, then no answer after two weeks had gone by; finally, in the third week, I got a reply. Dow agreed to come to Panama to marry me. I went to the travel agent in Panama but could not get them to send a ticket to Dow in Bangkok to come to Panama. Finally, I called the travel agent in Kansas and gave him all the information, and he agreed to send Dow her ticket to Bangkok where she could pick it up at the Japan Airlines office. Since I only had mail communications with Dow, I sent her the information on how to pick up her ticket at the airline office. I called Mom and Dad and told them Dow had agreed to come to Panama and marry me and that she should be in Panama on February 14. Dad was really happy I was getting married again and really liked Dow; however, Mom still seemed to have mixed emotions about the marriage.

I finally got the mimeographed orders from the Corp of Engineers, which would allow Dow to come to Panama. Since I only had mail contact with Dow, I had to send these by mail, too. Dow did not have an address or phone in Bangkok. I had to send all of her mail to one of her friends, who would pass the mail on to her. I had tried to get the Chase Manhattan Bank in Bangkok to give Dow extra money to travel to Panama. I had even sent additional money to the bank to give to Dow, but they would only give her the monthly allowance I had set up for her. The bank in Panama telexed the Bangkok bank to give Dow the extra money but they refused. I sent Dow a $100 bill for travel money in the envelope with the two copies of travel orders from the Corps of Engineers that will allow her to come to Panama to get married. I hoped I had covered all the bases. Dow could finally get her tickets from Japan Airlines to come to Panama and bring the travel orders as well as some money to travel with.

CHAPTER 22:
DOW'S PANAMA FLIGHT

With all of this done, Dow would be able to leave Bangkok on February 13, fly to Tokyo, then on to Los Angles, where she would get the flight to Panama and would arrive in Panama on February 14 at 7:00PM – Valentine's Day. I had only to wait for a few more days till Dow would arrive and we could get married. I picked out a set of wedding bands for us and paid for them. We only needed to get Dow's ring sized when she came. I got a lot of things I thought we would need to set up housekeeping in Panama while I was waiting. I had my camping kit we could use till Dow picked out the things she needed.

Valentine's Day arrived! I picked up a dozen red roses and a big box of Valentine chocolates to take with me to the airport for Dow. I could hardly wait for Dow's flight. I left early to go to the airport to get her, and I watched the flight come into the airport. Then I went to the arrival section to wait for Dow to come out of the baggage claim and customs area. I waited and waited and waited. Finally, I asked the people at the arrival area if everybody from the flight had checked through and they told me they had. I then went to the airlines and checked the passenger list and Dow was not on the list. The people at the airlines said this happened all of the time and she would surely be on the flight tomorrow night. They thought she may have been late coming from Tokyo or got held up at the airport and missed the outgoing flight, but would surely be on the flight tomorrow. I left the airport feeling very sad. I returned to my pick up and drove back to the hotel to get some sleep.

    The next day after work, I gathered up the roses and the box of chocolates again and headed back to the airport to pick up Dow. I arrived early and watch the flight land, waiting for Dow to get off the flight. All of the passengers got off the plane and I checked to make sure all of the passengers had passed through customs. Then I returned to the airline and checked the passenger list. Dow's name was not on it. I asked if they knew what could have happened, but they had no idea. I returned to my truck thinking maybe at the last minute Dow could have changed her mind.

    I called the travel agent where I got Dow's ticket to see what could have happened. He checked and found that Dow did pick up the ticket in Bangkok and did board the plane in Bangkok to come to Panama. He said he would check further to see if he could find what could have happened to her. I called Mom to tell her Dow had not arrived. When Mom answered, she told me that Dow had called her and she was in Los Angeles. However, she did not give her an address or a phone number where we could reach her. I told Mom if Dow called back, to try and get a phone number or an address and I would call back to find out what she had learned. I was sick; Dow was her family's main support – her parents and her children all depended on her for their support.

Chapter 23: The Search

The next morning, I went to the office and told the project manager I had to go to Los Angeles to find out what happened to Dow. I had already gotten a round trip ticket and had left the return date open. After telling the project manager, I left to go to the airport with just a carryon bag.

Before leaving for Los Angeles, I called Mom one more time to let her know I was going to Los Angeles to find Dow. Mom told me Dow had called again and had not given her a telephone number but would call later with one. I boarded my flight to Los Angeles. The plane seemed to take forever to get to Los Angeles. When we arrived, I went through immigration, and since I only had a carryon bag, customs should have been really easy – or *would* have been – except I was coming from the wrong part of the world and they searched my bag for drugs. With that over, I went out of the arrival gate and started my search.

I went to the airlines Dow was supposed to take to come to Panama. I went to the ticketing counter and gave them the flight number of Dow's flight and the travel date of February 14, along with a picture of Dow, to see if they could remember seeing her check in. After viewing the picture, they remembered her trying to check in. They said they could not let her board because she did not have a round trip ticket. I told them she did not need a round trip ticket because she had a set of orders, and I showed them a copy of the orders. They said Dow did not show them the orders, and since she did not have a round trip ticket, they could not let her take her scheduled flight. I asked them where Dow could have gone, but they did not know.

Since Dow had a two-entry visa for the U.S. in her passport, she could have entered the U.S. again. If she entered Los Angeles, where could she be? I went to the police station at the airport next, checking to see if they had any information on where Dow could be. I filled out a missing person's report; since she had been missing since February 14th, the police had no trouble accepting the report. I gave them Dow's arrival flight on Japan Airlines, the flight number and her onward flight number to Panama. I gave them a picture of Dow also. I told them I had gone to the airlines Dow was supposed to take to get to Panama to marry me, but they would not let her on the plane because she did not have a round trip ticket, and Dow did not show them the orders I had sent to her to allow her to come to Panama. The police officer asked me for an address where I was staying and a phone number. Of the police officers I talked to, one was a plainclothes policeman and the other a uniformed officer in training to become a detective. I told them I had just arrived from Panama and had not checked into a hotel yet. They suggested a reasonable hotel in the airport to me. I told them I would call them when I had checked in and give them the room and phone number. They gave me their phone number and the name of the man who would be handling the case.

Then I was at a dead end. I went to the hotel the police had suggested and checked in. I then called Mom to see if Dow had called again. Dow had called and wanted to know when I was going to come and pick her up and had given Mom a phone number. I wrote down the phone number, having Mom repeat it twice to make sure I had it correct. I then called the phone number. There was no answer. I called the police and told them Dow had called my Mom and had given Mom a phone number, which I gave to them. I told them I had called the number and there was no answer. They said they would check on the number to see if they could put an address to the number and said they would call me back later. They told me not to call that number anymore.

The police suggested that I go to Chinatown and search for Dow. They said that if they went, the Chinese would believe they were looking for her to deport her and they would not give the police any information. However, if somebody went looking for her that was not from the police, the people may help him. I got a taxi and went to Chinatown. First, I walked the streets looking for her, since Chinatown in L.A. was not as large as the one in San Francisco. When I could not find Dow by walking the streets, I started asking in the restaurants if they had seen Dow. I go from restaurant to restaurant showing them Dow's picture and asking them if they had seen her, leaving my name and phone number at the places that would take it, so if they saw Dow she could call me. I went to the grocery stores showing them Dow's picture and asking them if they had seen Dow. They all said that they had not seen her. As a last resort, I went to the jewelry stores showing them Dow's picture. When I entered one jewelry store, they looked at the picture and told me Dow was not Chinese. I told them she was Thai. Then they talked a lot in Chinese, and came back to me to tell me that there was a Thai Buddhist Temple not too far from there. Maybe if I went to the temple, they might have seen her. They gave me the address for the Thai Buddhist Temple.

I walked out of Chinatown and went to the main street to get a taxi. I gave him the address and we were off to the temple. When I got to the temple, I found a Buddhist monk. I gave him a picture of Dow and tried talking to him, but he did not speak any English. He led me into a small part of the temple that some people were just coming into, to a young Thai lady to whom he spoke in Thai. Then she turned to me and asked, "May I help you?"

"Yes," I said. "My finance has become lost in Los Angeles, while flying through from Bangkok, and I was hoping that maybe she would have come here and you may have seen her?"

"Do you have a picture of her?" she asked.

"Yes," I answered. "I have given it to the monk."

The Thai lady spoke to the monk in Thai, and the monk turned to me and handed me the picture back to show to the Thai lady. In the Buddhist religion, it was believed that women were unclean, and the monks could not be touched by women, so he would not pass the picture to the woman. I then passed the picture to the Thai lady to see if that she had seen Dow. After she looked at it, she passed it to the group of people with her. They all looked at the picture and shook their heads no, that they had not seen her. I thanked them and gave them my phone number at the hotel to call me if they saw Dow, and if they did see Dow, to tell her to call me. I got a taxi and returned to the hotel, very depressed, thinking of what else I could do to find Dow.

As a last resort, I called a newspaper to see if they would help me find Dow. They handled my call like I was some kind of crackpot and gave me a lot of "we will check on it for you and when we get enough information will put it in the paper and will call you back". I knew they would never call me back, because they never even asked me for my phone number. Then I tried to call another paper, hoping I could get some reporter interested in my story and help me by putting Dow's picture in the paper. I knew the longer I waited, the less chance I had to find her. They gave me the runaround and the same "we will call you back", but they never asked for my phone number either so I knew they would never call.

I called Dow's number again and again and could not get any answer. I realized I had not eaten all day and I was hungry, so I went downstairs and walked across the street to get a sandwich to eat, not caring about enjoying it, but just to fill me up.

I returned to the hotel and made a list of the things I knew and had done to try and to find Dow.

1. I know Dow made it to Los Angeles.
2. The airlines would not allow Dow on her connecting flight to Panama because she did not have a round trip ticket.
3. I have contacted the police to have them help me find Dow.
4. I have contacted the newspaper to help find Dow. No help.
5. I have a phone number that Dow has provided in Los Angles.
6. I have searched in Chinatown and the Thai Buddhist Temple and have left my phone number to call me.

I tried calling the newspapers again to see if I can get any help from them, but got the brush off from them again.

Just as I hung up, the police called me back. They had put an address to the phone number that Dow had given to Mom. They went to the address where the phone was located and said they had found Dow's luggage at the address but Dow was not there. They told me they would keep on checking to find her. The police would not give me the address where they went.

I thought I would try calling the number again. "Hello," a woman's voice says on the other end of the phone.

"Hello," I said, "I am Edwin Kime and my fiancée gave me this phone number where I could find her. I want to pick her up and get married."

"The police were just here looking for her," she told me. "Why did you call the police?"

"May I talk to Dow?" I asked. "I had called the police because I needed somebody to help me try and find her."

"She is not here now," the lady answered. "She will be here in the morning though."

"Then I will come and pick her up at 8:00AM in the morning," I said.

"I will help you find her, if you can give me some money, like $100." she said.

"I have a pencil and paper; please give me your address," I asked. The lady gave me an address, and I wrote it down and double checked with her to make sure it was correct.

"Don't forget to bring me the money," the woman said again.

"That's alright, I will give you the money when I find Dow," I told the lady. She told me the address again to make sure I had it correct. I would be there first thing in the morning, I told the lady again. When it was all agreed, the lady hung up.

I tried to sleep, but it was a long night. I kept checking the clock to make sure I had not slept too long, but the clock would only read fifteen minutes later than it had been the last time I had checked. Finally, at 5:00AM, I got up, as I could not sleep anyway. I shaved, cleaned up, and then got dressed. I went downstairs and got some breakfast.

After breakfast, I returned to my room. I thought I had better call the police. I called the police and, to my surprise, I got one of the officers I had talked to. I told him I had talked to the lady that was supposed to know where Dow was and I was going there to meet her and pick up Dow at 8:00AM this morning. The police said not to go, that it was too dangerous. I told them I was going; I had to get Dow. The police said there had been two murders recently in that area and it was just too dangerous. They said they could not go then but they would go when they could.

"You have already been there and not found her. I need to go to find her. Look," I told the police officer, "I am going to get Dow. When I return with Dow, I will call you and let you know everything is all right. If I don't call you back, you will know I did not make it."

The police told me again not to go there; it was just too dangerous and I could get killed. I told them I was going and before they could respond, I hung up.

I went downstairs and called a taxi. When the taxi arrived, I gave the driver the address and we started off. We were soon on the freeway, heading north. The meter kept clicking up the fare when he turned off of the freeway into a residential neighborhood. The drive seemed to last forever and the meter kept clicking. We kept passing streets in the housing project we had turned into. We finally came to the street name that was on the address I had, and the taxi driver turned left onto it. We went around a small curve and I spotted the house number. The taxi driver then pulled to a stop in front of the house number I had. I asked the taxi driver to wait for me, that I had to pick up my fiancée and her luggage and we would leave. I climbed out of the taxi and walked up toward the house. A middle-aged lady was waiting in the driveway for me. She had the look of a lady you would expect to find in a Nazi military photo, not the look of a middle-aged housewife.

"Where is Dow?" I asked the lady.

"She is not here now," the lady answered, then continued: "She should be back at any time; did you bring me the money?"

"I will give you the money when I have Dow," I told the lady. My heart was sad; what had happen to Dow? Had this lady killed her and only left the suitcases in her house? Where was Dow? The lady kept backing toward the garage as I kept moving toward her. Although she was really mean looking, she seemed to be afraid of what I might do to her if I got my hands on her. Just at that time, Dow came walking around the curve. I ran to meet her, grabbing her and kissing and hugging her. I had been afraid I would never see her again.

"Dow, get into the taxi and let's leave," I told Dow.

"No, no!" she said, "I have to get my luggage."

I did not care about her luggage; I just wanted to get her in the taxi and go to someplace that was safe. We could always get her new things. Dow insisted on getting her luggage. I went with her and we picked up her luggage. All the time we were getting Dow's luggage, the lady kept asking me for money, like a leach sticking to me. When we finally got all of Dow's luggage put into the taxi, the lady was waiting with her hand out. I knew I should not have given her any money, but I did. To my surprise, when I gave her the money, instead of asking for more, she said, "Thank you". We climbed into the taxi and drove back to the hotel and safety.

The long ride back to the hotel seemed to last only a short time compared with the ride out there. I held Dow's hand; I did not want to lose contact with her again. Dow had gotten mad because I had given the lady some money. She said she had already paid her. Dow then went on to tell me the lady was a taxi driver and worked at night. So Dow would sleep at night when she worked. Then during the day she would walk around town when the lady was at home. She did not know why she came back to the house this morning, but I was sure glad she did.

I showed Dow the set of orders I had sent to her. She told me she had never gotten the orders. We searched for the answer to this problem. Finally, I remembered the address I had sent all of Dow's mail to, including the orders, was not Dow's but one of her friend's. What must have happened was that when her friend got the letter, she opened it. Like most Thais, she opened any mail that came to her. The lady found the $100 bill and knew what it was and kept it. Not being able to read English, she did not know what the orders said and believed they were not important. Or maybe someone in the post office had opened the envelope, taken the money, and thrown the orders away. We did not know what had happened, but we did know that Dow did not get the orders, even though all of my other letters had gotten through to Dow. We suspected that Dow's friend did not give her the letter so she could keep the $100 that was in it. When we arrived at the hotel, we unloaded Dow's luggage. I paid and thanked the taxi driver. He really didn't know what had happened or why I thanked him, and seemed kind of startled when I did.

We took Dow's luggage to my room. When we there, I called the police to tell them I had found Dow. They told me again how dangerous it was to go out there, that I could have been shot and killed, or gotten Dow killed. I told them lots of things could have happened, but what *had* happened was that I now had Dow. We were going to get plane tickets and go to Panama and get married. I thanked the police for their help and they said they were glad it had ended so happily. Then I hung up. Next, I called my parents to tell them I had found Dow.

We walked over to the airline ticket office with which I had my ticket to get a confirmed flight back to Panama tomorrow. We also had Dow's ticket with us. I asked the lady if she could get us together on the same flight. She listened to what had happened with Dow. She then called her supervisor. Her supervisor called the airline Dow was supposed to fly on and they agreed to transfer the ticket so Dow could fly with me on the flight to Panama tomorrow.

When all of this was done, we were very hungry. It had been a long morning. We went to the airport restaurant to eat a very late lunch. The airport restaurant was on a suspended platform above the building, and we could watch the planes as they came in to land and take off as we ate. We were high enough to see for a long way when the air was clear. The meal was a celebration of finding Dow.

Lunch over, Dow wanted to get some souvenirs at the souvenir shops by the airport. Dow always took her time shopping, and when she was finished, we returned to the hotel. I wrote to the two newspapers and told them that I had found Dow and put my address in Panama on the letters. We never did get any reply from them. They were not concerned about things like that – only what happened to movie stars and celebrities.

We showered and freshened up at the hotel. It had been a long day for us and we were tired. I had not really slept since Dow had become lost. We sorted through and packed the things Dow had bought, getting Dow's suitcases ready for the trip to Panama tomorrow. When we were finished, we were so tired we just went downstairs and ate in the hotel restaurant. However, I had brought a bottle of champagne with me for us to celebrate our getting back together. When we finished eating and drinking, we were really tired, and the champagne relaxed us and made us ready for bed. We could get good night's sleep that night being together.

In the morning, we rose late, got cleaned up, dressed, and went downstairs for breakfast. When we finished breakfast, we returned to our room to complete our packing. We then took the luggage downstairs and checked out of the hotel. We got a taxi for the short distance from the hotel to the terminal. We unloaded at the terminal and made our way to the check-in counter, checking into the same airline so Dow could not get lost again. We got our boarding passes and got Dow's luggage checked through to Panama. With that done, we headed for the boarding gate.

On the way to the boarding gate, we met the plain-clothes officer and another officer who had worked to help me find Dow. He looked a lot different then since he was wearing a uniform. I introduced him to Dow. He questioned why the two of us were leaving Los Angeles so quickly. Then he answered his own question, saying, "With all the trouble and problems you two have had in Los Angeles, I can understand why you want to leave." Then he added that most of the people in Los Angeles were not bad, and asked us to not let this one bad experience make us think all people from Los Angeles were bad, and that he was sure happy I had found Dow and that nobody was hurt. Then we parted from the two policemen.

We walked to the boarding gate area and were seated, waiting for the boarding call. They called the boarding for our flight to Panama, and it did not matter now how long the flight took, since we were back together. We boarded the plane and found our assigned seats. We stored our carryon luggage and were soon ready for our flight. The plane was pushed away from the boarding gate and we were taxing to the runway. The sky was clear as we reached the runway and began our takeoff. In a short time, we were airborne and on our way to Panama.

We had our lunch aboard the flight to Panama, and soon we were making our descent to the Panama airport. We felt the wheels touch down on the runway at Panama; we had finally made it! The plane taxied to the unloading gate area and came to the sudden bumpy stop. The doors were opened and we disembarked at the Panama airport.

This time, we made our way to the U.S. Immigration section. I gave the Immigration Officer Dow's and my passports and the set of orders for Dow. I explained to the Immigration Officer that Dow had come to marry me and got lost in Los Angeles and I had to go get her. He then stamped our passports and we proceeded on to the baggage claim area, finding our luggage. We went through the U.S. customs section and were finally out of the airport. I had Dow wait for me in front of the airport while I went to get the pickup. I pulled up in front of the airport, loaded up the luggage, and we were finally headed to our hotel.

It took us only a short time to reach our hotel in Panama City. When we reached the hotel, we took our luggage up to our room. When we reached the room, I gave Dow the much-delayed Valentine chocolates. Then I ran downstairs to get her a dozen red roses. I brought them back to give to her; so finally she had the things I had wanted to give her when she was supposed to arrive on Valentine's Day, 1979.

We went downstairs and ate supper, after which we returned to the room, showered and cleaned up. We were both tired. Also, I had to go to work early in the morning.

In the morning, I arose early and let Dow sleep because she was so tired. I fixed myself some breakfast, then was off to work. I had been away only three days, but had to spend the next couple of days catching up at work.

I got the paperwork started for Dow and I to get married in the U.S. Panama Canal Section. When it was completed, we just needed to set the date. I sent out announcements that we were getting married to my parents, my sister, and our friends. We spent the next few days gathering things we would need after we got married.

CHAPTER 24: THE MARRIAGE

I finally had all the paperwork needed to get married. I had written Larry and told him I was going to get married, like I had promised I would. We had promised that the first one of us to marry would tell the other one before they did it. It was a local holiday time in Panama, like Mardi Gras in New Orleans; they had parades, costumes, and threw water. All of the local workers were on holiday. I went to the government offices in the Canal Zone and picked up the paperwork we needed for our marriage on February 26, 1979. To get married, we needed two witnesses. I searched everywhere to find two people from the company that would stand up for us to witness our marriage, but everybody was out on holiday. I finally found Bonner Davis, our new business manager, and John Boatwright, and got them to come down to the courthouse where the judge would marry us. I took Dow aside and told her while we were still in the pickup, before the four of us went into the judge's chambers to take my hand because I knew Dow would not be able to understand the way the judge talked.

"So when it gets to the part in the wedding ceremony where the judge says to you, 'do you take this man to be your husband', I will squeeze your hand and you will need to say 'yes, I do'." Then we were ready to go into the judge's chambers and be married.

Dow was dressed in new white slacks and a new white ruffled blouse trimmed in gold. She was wearing the gold chain with the medallion I had given her when I returned to Thailand from Saudi Arabia. She had a blue headband in her black hair and a borrowed old fish sticker on her blouses collar from me. She was dressed in white and gold like a bride should be, and she looked stunning and ready for a wedding. We had to use the engagement ring I had given to Dow for our marriage, because the correct sized matching wedding bands still had not come back. So she had something old, something new, something borrowed, and something blue.

The four of us entered the judge's chambers and gave the judge the required paperwork to get married as well as the engagement ring to use during the wedding ceremony. The judge started the ceremony and went through all the parts, then he came to the end of the ceremony and asked Dow, "Do you take this man to be your wedded husband?"

When he said that, I squeezed Dow's hand, and Dow said, "Yes, I do." Then we proceeded with the wedding ceremony. Finally, I placed the ring on Dow's finger and the wedding ceremony was over. I kissed Dow and we were finished. Finally we were married!

Then the judge turned to me and said, "I do not believe Dow understood a word that I said."

I squeezed Dow's hand again and she said, "Yes, I do."

The judge shook his head and then got a very puzzled look on his face. He signed and stamped the marriage license and marriage certificate then passed them to Bonner Davis and to John Boatwright to witness by signing the marriage certificate to complete the paperwork.

We were married in the United States Panama Canal Section on February 26, 1979. I returned to work in the afternoon. Dow went with me as we drove to Colon that afternoon to look at some work on our projects there. Colon was on the Atlantic side and we were on the Pacific side (Panama City) of the isthmus, so it was a fifty-mile drive across the isthmus close to the canal and over one bridge to Colon. At the bridge, the locals were selling peacock bass. When we returned, we bought some to take back to the hotel with us. Later, we used the rods and reels we had bought in Pittsburg to catch these wonderful fish in the canal and in the surrounding lakes.

That night after work, we went out by ourselves to celebrate our wedding. The other people from the company were all too busy celebrating the holiday to celebrate with us.

We soon started working to get Dow her U.S. citizenship. We also brought her children to the U.S. to get their education. Sadly, Dad passed away in April 1979 without ever getting to meet his three new grandkids or play with them. But the joyful irony in all of this was that I had gone to Bangkok to find a friend I had made in Viet Nam, and instead found myself a wife.